MW01101736

TARGET

Also by Kathleen Jeffrie Johnson

The Parallel Universe of Liars

TARGET

Kathleen
Jeffrie
Johnson

A DEBORAH BRODIE BOOK
Roaring Brook Press
Brookfield, Connecticut

A Deborah Brodie Book
Published by Roaring Brook Press
A Division of The Millbrook Press
2 Old New Milford Road
Brookfield, Connecticut 06804

LIBRARY OF CONGRESS CATALOGING-IN-PUBLICATION DATA

Johnson, Kathleen Jeffrie.
 Target / Kathleen Jeffrie Johnson.—1st ed.
   p. cm.
"A Deborah Brodie Book."
Summary: After being raped, Grady goes to a new high school where he meets an
outgoing African American and several other students who try to help him deal with
the horrible secret.
 [1. Rape—Fiction. 2. Anorexia nervosa—Fiction. 3. Race
relations—Fiction. 4. Homosexuality—Fiction. 5. High schools—Fiction. 6.
Schools—Fiction.] I. Title.
 PZ7.J6324Tar 2003
 [Fic]—dc21
                                        2003008574
First edition

10 9 8 7 6 5 4 3 2 1
ISBN 0-7613-1932-8 (trade hard cover)

10 9 8 7 6 5 4 3 2 1
ISBN 0-7613-2790-8 (library binding)

Book design by Jaye Zimet
Printed in the United States of America

"Let's dance!" said he.
"Okay!" said she.
And off they went.

Thanks to those who have invited me to the dance.
Wild Bartholomew
Wolfgrrl
Deborah Brodie
Tracey Adams

TARGET

Tackled from the rear, Grady buckled, pitching forward to the ground—his arms grabbed and jerked back and up. The man who had asked for directions yanked him by the hair—his damned hair—then slammed him across the nose, shoving him down, grinding his face into the walk. Grady felt his wrists being tied, felt his head jerked up once more. Smelling alcohol on the man's breath, he found himself staring at a dim, stubbled face. Tape was slapped across his mouth, and then he met the sidewalk again, someone's knee pushing against the back of his neck, forcing skin off his cheek.

He was so astonished by all this, so surprised, that fear didn't find him right away. He didn't even feel present, as if this were a scene in a movie he was watching—he'd paid his money, he'd come to see a good action flick. But then he tasted something acrid in his mouth—blood—and fear, like a crazed, inarticulate beast, woke up. He started to scream, but couldn't, his mouth was taped shut.

He'd been hunted and downed in minutes. As big as he was, he'd long ago let his *danger* alert go off-line, and stopped paying attention. And tonight, when he'd chosen to walk home alone from Tracy's concert, taking the loop down dark and isolated Manchester Avenue, he *really* wasn't paying attention. So when a man climbed out of the passenger side of a van and asked him for directions, he'd carelessly stopped to answer.

Now one of the men grabbed hold of Grady's hair again, using it to haul him to his knees. Silent, his face a harsh blur, the man slapped him once, twice—and Grady felt his skin split, felt his eye slam shut, then try to pry itself back open. The man kicked him in the gut and Grady's insides exploded. Then they dragged him over to the van and shoved him in the back.

Easy.

Trapped and bound.

He was theirs to have.

TWO

No one here knew. That's all that mattered.

Grady sat in the passenger seat of his mother's Honda Accord and stared at the brick front of Thomas Jefferson High, his new school. Old, ugly, and sprawling, the building ranged in color from deep red to rust to orange. Grady had noticed the variable color scheme as they drove up. Probably, if you were so inclined, you could study the brick and figure out where additional wings and rooms and hallways had been added on over the years to accommodate more students.

Grady wasn't so inclined.

A large, square auditorium stood at the far end, its orange facade bright and new. The acoustics were probably pretty good for concerts and plays, not like at his old school, Delmont High, where voices had to be really good to soar past the lousy construction. Tracy's voice had been good enough. But Grady hadn't heard her sing in a long time. Like his other friends, she was a part of his past that no longer existed.

He'd left extracurricular events, along with his friends, several miles behind. He had transferred to Jefferson to take classes, to pass. Nothing else.

He watched as kids disappeared into the building, moving in streams through the row of front doors. Other kids hung back, probably doing the same thing Grady was doing: waiting till the last moment. Why rush? He'd wait until most of the kids were in, until just enough lingered around the entrance that he could hide among them, not be pushed or shoved as he might be in a crowd. Not be touched. He'd be just another guy among a couple dozen guys—girls, too, of course—finally moving into the school, ready to look for his homeroom, his locker, trying not to feel nervous. Showing up for another start of another school year.

Except this one was different.

"Grady?"

"Hmm?" He turned and looked at his mother, his head brushing the inside roof of the car. She sat in the driver's seat, her hands still clutching the steering wheel, poised to turn, as if she hadn't parked—illegally—in the turnaround in front of the school ten minutes ago, hadn't turned the engine off.

"Getting out?" She wore her worried look, her *Is Everything Okay?* look. As of yesterday, her hair was now a reddish brown and stuck out in short swoops and curls all over her head. She kept changing it, as if that would make all her problems go away.

Grady frowned. He kept his own hair cut in a way low buzz, his father doing the honors for him with an old pair of clippers. He didn't see why his mother didn't just let her hair go gray, if that's what it was doing. Everyone was always trying to change things that couldn't be changed. She was an adult. She should know better.

"Grady? Do you want to wait until after the bell and have me go in with you? You know, just to the front office? I could say it took longer to get here in rush hour than I expected."

"Mom!"

She twisted her lips and sighed, stared out through the windshield.

Cripes. All he needed was to win the Weenie Award by walking into school holding his mother's hand—all six feet, three inches of him. He might be a waste, but there was no need to advertise it. "I'm going now, okay?" His voice came out dry and cracked; he just didn't talk much anymore, he was out of practice. Besides, what was there to say? Opening the car door, he gathered up his backpack, then felt his mother's hand on his arm.

"It'll be fine, Grade." She hesitated, leaving her hand on his arm a moment longer than strictly necessary, as if searching out the memory of their old closeness. He allowed it, feeling her lightly rub her fingers over the material of his long-sleeved shirt, the shirt he wore to hide his thinness. Then he abruptly pulled away. Probably she was just trying to measure his arm, determine if he'd lost any more weight.

"Grady, try to eat your lunch today, okay?"

He nodded briefly, and climbed out.

School.

It was supposed to be his senior year, but it wasn't. He had to start eleventh grade all over again. It was supposed to be his old high school, but it wasn't. It was supposed to be—well, what? A different life, that's what. Well, too bad about that, this was *After*. That's life, is that how the song went? That old song, the one by Frank Sinatra or somebody, the one his mother hummed under her breath when she was trying not to show how anxious she was? The one she had hummed all the way to school this morning? Jesus Christ. His mother wasn't *that* old. Sinatra was from the dark ages, not to mention dead. Good music for somebody's grandmother, maybe.

His mother started up the Honda and pulled away. He knew she'd be late for work. She did bookkeeping and general office work for a small catering service that was trying hard to become a large catering service, and attendance was not optional.

He stood still, feeling the early September air envelop him in leftover summer heat. For one moment, he felt as if he'd made it all the way to school without trouble, without feeling his balls tighten and reach for his stomach, without feeling the back of his throat start to constrict, without feeling his breakfast start its acid crawl toward his mouth.

He became aware that he was out in the open, that he stood out, that he had to move, get among a bunch of kids. Not close enough that anyone might touch him, but close enough that he wouldn't be so *seen.*

Fear scrambled up the back of his throat. One step, he told himself. One step to start. He pushed his left foot forward, then swung his weight to the right. He could do this. The tension in his throat began to ease. This step. That step. Simple. He continued all the way to one of the front doors. This hand opening the door. That hand holding it open for the next person.

Easy.

He was in.

One empty desk remained at the back of homeroom. He'd be safe there, his back protected. Grady rushed for it, pushing across, plowing between a bunch of kids still cruising for seats, trampling a small black kid aiming for the same desk, all but shoving him aside.

"You fuckhead!" the boy shouted, turning heads, burning his anger directly into Grady's eyes. His dreads looked like the thick black legs of a spider. "So much for improved race relations, *honkey*-butt!"

Honkey-butt? *You fucking n—* Grady wrestled rage out of his head, wrestled the word away from his mouth. Silent, his face burning, he stared at the black kid, then stared at the floor, ashamed. He never used to talk like that.

"Problem there?" The teacher gazed across the room over his bifocals.

The boy glared at Grady and sniffed loudly, then turned to the teacher. "Naw. We're just getting acquainted." He thumped down in the seat in front of the desk Grady had won, opened a black-and-white composition book, and proceeded to ignore everyone.

Grady, his hands shaking, sweat coating his upper lip, sat down at the prized desk and tried to calm himself. The day was just beginning and he'd already made an enemy—a *black* guy, for

Christ's sake. How would he make it to three o'clock? He swallowed hard, tried to focus on where he was, but the room and the kids and the teacher started to blur.

He made himself breathe. *This* breath, in, for calm and quiet, for still water—for new beginnings. Well, that's why he was here, right? *That* breath, out, for what had already passed—his old school, his old friends. For what would never be again. Measuring his breaths helped steady him. He felt tension slip a bit from his shoulders, let go of his arms.

He swallowed, let his eyes fall shut.

The teacher started taking roll. Grady blinked his eyes open, readied himself to hear his own name. Some kids grunted, "Here," or "Present," in response, others merely raised a hand. That's what he would do—wave; his voice didn't work too well. He ran his fingers over the smooth top of his desk. He had to do this right, that was the deal; come back to school and do it, wave his hand when he had to, come back and—

"Grady West?"

His hand plunged into his lap, then banged the underside of his desk as he tried to pull it back up. Somehow he managed to stick it up in the air, knuckles scraped. The teacher nodded, made a mark in his book.

Relieved, Grady let his hand slide back down to his lap. Done—that hadn't been so hard. Sweat prickled his skin, and he shivered. He was cold all the time now, he should have brought a sweater. He stuck his fingers between his legs.

"Oh. West. This is for you."

Grady watched the teacher hand a white envelope to the student sitting at the front of his row, watched the envelope travel head over hand until it landed with the black guy in front of him: Dreadlock Central. The kid turned around, and, when Grady didn't take it right away, waved the envelope in his face. "Wake up, chalk boy. I got more important things to do than deliver your mail. Slave days are over."

Grady woke up. He took the envelope and the kid turned around.

He stared at it a moment, reading over and over his name printed on the front. Then, glancing around to see if anyone was watching—no one was—he carefully opened it, pulling out a single sheet of paper.

"Welcome New Student!" it said across the top. Then, below, "The *Jefferson Journal*, your school newspaper, wants to know who you are! Where do you come from? What school did you last attend? What are your plans for this year, what are your interests? Okay—yada yada yada—you get the idea, right? Fill out the information below and drop it off in Room 107, or use our email address at the bottom of the page. The *Journal* will highlight one (interesting!) new student in each issue for the next couple of months. Then, the student voted *most interesting* by our readers gets a prize! So let's get to know you, okay? Let's get really real!"

Grady refused the tension rising like a thick syrup through his limbs. He carefully folded the piece of paper in half, then half again, then again and again, until it was a fat little wedge of nothing. At the end of homeroom, on his way out the door, he dropped it in the trash can.

Nobody here knew him.

And nobody would.

THREE

Grady stopped at his locker before lunch, a clutch of books in his arms. So far, his classes had gone okay, but he really needed to go home, lie down, sleep. The day, though, was only half over. He still had lunch, then more classes. He had to remain upright that long. Longer, because then he had to—

"Hey, *you*, chalk boy!"

Grady spun around, slamming against his locker, almost dropping the books in his arms.

A brown face surrounded by a clump of dreadlocks glared up at him. "Next time you need to stomp a guy first thing in the morning, pick somebody else, okay? I don't take that kind of shit from *no* one." His dark eyes burned.

Crap. The guy from homeroom. Grady's stomach knotted. He pressed his lips together, trying not to feel sick.

His composition book tucked under his arm, the boy opened the locker next to Grady's. "Well, fate and all that. Lockers together and everything." He turned to Grady. "I know, we can be homeroom *pals*, overcome our racial division as we struggle to get along. Get written up in the *Jefferson Journal*, go on national TV and hold hands, sing 'Kumbayah.' You game, boy?"

No. He wasn't game at all. Sweat prickled Grady's armpits.

The kid laughed and shook his head, stuffing some books in his locker. "Just jump right in when you feel the need to apologize." He rubbed his nose. "I can handle it. I deal with jerks of all colors, races, and creeds, but I'm especially good with Caucasians." He looked at Grady and smiled. "I'm one of the few brothers currently available for decent conversation in this oh-so-white school of ours, so I suggest you take advantage of the opportunity." He reached into his locker, rummaging around for something.

Grady swallowed. "Um." Kids flowed past them down the halls. He tried to ignore them, remain calm, but his hands shook. Okay. Apologize. That was fair. He'd practically bulldozed this guy. And he'd almost used the *n*-word—maybe the kid knew it, had sniffed it out. Grady ran a fingertip over the cover of one of his books, struggling to find his voice. "S—." His voice cracked. "S-sorry." There. Done. He licked his lips.

The boy glanced up at Grady. "Not even gonna cop an *I didn't mean it, I'm really not prejudiced* plea? Damn. I expected more from you than that."

He waited. Grady said nothing.

"Little short on the conversational skills, I see. All right, I'll cover—conversation is my specialty." He studied Grady a moment. "I'm Jess. Nice name, don't you think?" He chewed his lip, surveying Grady as if he were a city block in need of renovation. Grady closed his eyes, bringing the books in his arms up to his chest, holding them tight.

His fingers explored the edge of one, then the cover. Hard and smooth, soothing in its smoothness. From its small size, it was probably the book from his English class. His fingers traveled to another one. Cool, a bit rougher to the touch, but also comforting. It was thicker, probably Botany. Feeling himself relax just a bit, Grady opened his eyes, taking in the pale light of the hallway.

"You in need of medical assistance? I hate to say this, but you look kinda mental up there. Not to dis the psychos among us or anything." The boy scratched his shoulder on the opened door of his locker. "Hey, you don't have to worry about *me*, if that's the problem. I'm not one of those *bad* boys. I ain't gonna steal your lunch money." He turned to his locker and reached his arm in, thrashing around. "Shit. Where is it?"

Grady watched him press his face against the narrow opening

of his locker, rummage further, then pull out a paperback. Grady tried to read the title. *Notes of a Native Son.* Baldwin.

"There. Sucker tried to disappear on me. Figures. It's just like pussy, you know? Right when you think you got your hand on some, you don't." The boy flipped open the book and studied something, then shut it. He dug a finger down through his dreads and scratched. "I'm just so damn good at talking to white folk I get going and can't stop myself. End up talking to suckers like you." He slammed his locker shut, turned to face Grady fully, and smiled. "Nothing personal."

Grady tried to reengage his mind. It had frozen several sentences back, on the *p*-word. That was one word he refused to say, even to himself. He swallowed, trying to keep up with this Jess person, to not feel so frightened, so *mental*—but he had talked to no one besides his mother and father for months. He couldn't begin to know what to say to this guy.

"You still with me? Maybe I should call the nurse? If she's the same one they had coming around last year she's definitely all right. Nice tits. Think she'd give mouth-to-mouth to a brother?"

"I'm, uh . . . ." Grady flushed, holding his books tighter. He shut his eyes, then made himself open them, made himself shape his lips to speak. "I'm"—he swallowed hard—"okay." He had it now, he could talk, no need for a nurse. "You startled me." Easy.

"And *me* is? I don't remember the world's skinniest bean pole's name."

Grady blinked. This guy was making fun of him. He made himself look directly at the boy's face. Black. African American. Dreadlocks. They weren't real long, just down past his collar, and were actually kind of neat and tidy. There was nothing wrong with dreads, except—

He trembled slightly. They'd be so easy to grab hold of, pull you down with. Didn't this kid know that? He made himself take in the rest of the boy. He had a slight build, stood only five-five or -six maybe. His skin was a medium brown, his eyes a dark brown, almost black. The lips were generous, the mouth wide. He wore a T-shirt that said "Kiss My Black A—." Baggy jeans.

"Name? Unless you really are one of those racist jerks, in which case I'll have to find some other white person to harass." The boy's eyes flashed.

"G-Grady," he stammered. "Grady West."

"West! That's right. I'm Williams. Jess Williams. Now, Jess West might have been all right. It has a certain, um, sound and direction to it, don't you think? Maybe I should talk to your parents about adopting me." The boy's eyebrows lifted and his eyes glittered, daring Grady to take offense. But his mouth had its own thing going, holding something ready just offstage. A smile?

Grady felt something like a smile tease his own lips. It felt strange. His entire face— his entire *head*—felt slightly out of control. "Uh," he said, but Jess was moving off.

"Catch you later, Grady West. Gotta girl I gotta see." He started down the hall.

"Um."

The boy called back over his shoulder. "You might want to check your fly."

Grady spun to face his locker, dropping his books on the floor in his hurry to check. He blushed furiously, his hands groping, hoping no one could see what he was doing. His fingers found his zipper. Closed. Zipped. Shut tight.

Idiot. He stooped to pick up his books, then looked to see the back of Jess's head disappear around a corner, dreads stirring. Grady stood up, felt a rush of dizziness, and leaned against the wall.

His head cleared, and a smile reached his lips. Got him. The Jess-kid had gotten him.

He almost laughed, and looked back down the hall. It was empty now, all the kids had moved on. He leaned against the wall a moment longer, moving his lips silently, practicing the word he didn't say when the kid left.

Bye.

FOUR

A few minutes later, in the cafeteria line, Grady moved as invisibly as possible into a group of girls deciding on pizza squares or hamburgers, figuring none of them would get close enough to bump into him and touch him, even accidentally.

He waited patiently as the girls filled their trays, finally noticing a piece of paper taped to one of the plastic shields that ran along the serving line.

"Hey!" it read. "New Student! This is for you! Fill out the form you got in homeroom, or just drop by #107 and do some talky-talk stuff. Cooperate! Don't forget, the most interesting new student gets a prize! (We'll let you know *what* just as soon as we get enough money to buy something.) Identify yourself. Thrill us! Tell us your story!"

Grady moved forward with the girls, filing out in a line, and buying a carton of milk on the way.

His story. *Right.*

Headline: Grady West Buys Milk.

He found an empty table way over in the corner and sat down with his back to the wall, wishing he'd brought his portable CD player and his CDs, the ones that turned him, at least for a while, into a different person. He opened a book, pretending to read, and felt the tension in his shoulders begin to subside.

He got down half the carton of milk before his throat jammed up on him and he started to gag. He sat still, jaw clenched, willing his throat to relax. He carefully folded the lid shut and set the carton aside.

Enough of that.

* * *

Kids sat at the tables in clumps, scrunched close to friends. Other kids roamed between the rows of tables looking for someone they knew—all of them talking and yelling, the cafeteria in constant, noisy motion.

Just a year ago he'd sat with friends like that at Delmont. He'd sat with his Group, the kids he'd known since grade school, the six of them sticking together: his best buddy, Ted, plus Christian and Mikey-Mike the Mike, aka Mike, and of course the Two Girl-Ones, Clara-bell and Tracy.

Grady remembered his last lunch with them. How could he forget? It was the beginning of November, a year ago, a Friday. The last day of *Before*. It was incredibly mild out, almost balmy. The Group sat on the crinkly brown and yellow leaves scattered across the lawn, dining on a feast of ice-cream sandwiches, licking melting ice cream off their fingers. Tracy ended up with a little crumb of chocolate cake wedged in the corner of her mouth, right where her lips met.

Mikey-Mike shouted, *Hey, Trace, chocolate mouth!* And Tracy had blushed deeply, her face turning scarlet.

Grady had wanted to reach with his hand and feel Tracy's hot face, cool it off. He didn't understand why she was so embarrassed. She always looked fine to him. She sang in the chorus and he always went to her programs. They all did, unless they were going out. Ted, up to his eyeballs in girlfriends, was always going out.

That night they were attending one of her concerts—everyone except Ted, that is, and Christian, who was chasing some girl he'd never get. Clara-bell, the only one among them who had her own car—a used, badass yellow Firebird, red-and-black trim—was picking him and Mikey-Mike up. Tracy had a solo, and Grady looked forward to it. He liked to watch her sing, liked to watch her blond hair shine under the stage lights. He would have been happy to watch her just stand there, but he was careful not to let it show.

He was careful to just be friends.

That last lunch, the Two Girl-Ones plotted Clara-bell's next conquest, a guy in her Biology class named Hero. Mikey-Mike, shaking his crazy mop of rust-brown hair, said she could get him for sure just by bending over next to his desk and giving him a good look at her buns, get it, ha ha, *buns, hero, sandwich*? Everyone groaned.

Christian, laughing, smoothed back his straight-as-a-stick brown hair, all the while checking out every chick that passed. Tracy glanced at Christian, but never said anything, thought nobody noticed. Grady noticed, though. He noticed a lot of things, and not just about Tracy, although he noticed Tracy especially. He knew she liked Christian. He knew Christian didn't know.

Ted decided the chick leaning against the big oak tree across from them liked Grady and was sending him love vibes. Ted always gave Grady updates and reports on which girls wanted him, said he was trying to beef up Grady's sex life, told him girls *liked* him and he should take advantage of that fact.

Grady knew girls liked him. Girls liked him a lot.

Or used to.

Once upon a time, a boy had liked him, too. Trevor. But Grady hadn't liked him that way, just hadn't. The boy never said anything, never approached him, but Grady knew. Somehow, from the way the boy would glance at him, his face filled with a sad, quick longing, he knew. It had frightened him. It frightened him now. He'd never told anyone.

Grady read the word *pasteurized* on the carton of milk. Did it mean something, that a boy had once liked him? This was *After*. Now nothing meant what it used to.

* * *

Girls didn't mean the same thing now, either.

The day he turned twelve, he'd looked sixteen, his body already tall and strong and filled out. He sometimes wished he'd stayed like Ted, who remained small and hairless while Grady's body mounted its own personal space program and launched itself toward a new frontier. Ted had envied him, but Grady got nervous when girls "accidentally" brushed their breasts against his arm when they stood close to him and talked. He'd liked it, liked the way it felt, but what was he supposed to do about it? Ted would shake his head in disgust. How could he waste so many great opportunities?

But Ted caught up. With his dark, curly hair, hazel eyes, easy good looks, and quick grin, he became the first guy in their group to score, and his list of conquests kept growing. He didn't treat girls badly. He just knew what he wanted and, girl willing, went for it, keeping a steady supply of condoms handy. By now, all the guys knew to come to him in an emergency.

There was always another girl for Ted. They loved him.

Grady, the kid with the body, hung back.

Ted said he needed to get moving, get *laid*. Mikey-Mike had finally scored, and Christian would be coming in for a landing any day now. Shoot, Ted said, Clara-bell had done the Big Boink, and she hadn't been shy about letting them know, either. How could Grady let himself be outdone by a girl?

As for Tracy, well, Tracy *was* shy about things like that, blushing a thousand shades of red. They left her alone.

But Grady wasn't a fast mover like Ted. He'd only managed to touch a girl's breasts once. Mikey-Mike had dragged him to a party over a year ago, where the parents were out of town. Afraid to drink anything himself, he stood pinned to the wall, watching Mikey-Mike, along with about a million other kids, none of whom he knew, get plastered, and then make out. One couple rolling around in the corner decided to go ahead and plunge the poker, and Grady got his first demonstration of Live Sex. Watching, his body temperature shot up, and his dick began to hip-hop in his pants.

He became aware that a girl was standing next to him, also watching. *Christ.* He shifted his weight, trying to will his woody back down. Did it show?

Moot point.

Smelling of beer, she grabbed his shirt and pulled his face down, thrusting her tongue in his mouth. All but tackling him, she dragged him into a bedroom where she immediately pulled off her shirt and bra and planted her breasts in his hands and her tongue back in his mouth. Finding himself cupping a real set of knockers for the first time astonished him. His body shrieked with happiness, he wanted to push on, consume every part of her with his mouth, plant himself so deeply in her body there'd be no getting back out—but suddenly his stomach twisted sharply, his throat tightened, and he had to push her away. He fled outside, where—the only sober kid present—he threw up all over the azaleas.

A party fun fact he kept to himself.

Before, his sex life had consisted of jerking off. Alone. *After*, he couldn't even do that. Real sex with a real person—that was something he couldn't even imagine.

That was another planet.

FIVE

A kid tore past his table, yelling something. Grady jerked, remembering where he was: sitting by himself in the cafeteria at Thomas Jefferson High, his new school.

He looked around through the acre of kids. Spotting the Jess-guy, he felt a rush of recognition, then stifled it. Like they'd really sing "Kumbayah" together.

Actually, there weren't a whole lot of African-American kids around, not like at his old school. He watched Jess walk up to a black chick sitting at a table across from two other black girls. The girl's hair was sculpted upward into tall dark curls tinged with blonde. Grady had never understood how black girls got their hair so *arranged*. How did it stay put?

He watched Jess lean down and slide his arm around the girl's shoulder, at the same time helping himself to the empty chair beside her. At first the girl looked at him like, *Excuse me?*, but a second later, she was smiling. A classic Ted move.

He hadn't talked to Ted since that last lunch.

The noise in the room swelled with the clang of silverware banging against dishes and tables, plastic trays hitting the metal rollers in the food line, dishes slammed against tabletops. With shouting voices.

Letting his mind go blank, Grady finally realized he was staring at a girl seated a couple tables away with a bunch of other girls, a good-looking girl, and she was staring back at him. He dropped his eyes, studied his book, then glanced back up. She winked at him and laughed, her long, dark hair swinging over the side of her face as she half-turned to one of her friends and whispered something. Her hair swung back as she turned again to Grady and giggled.

Did she know, is that why she was laughing at him? Was she telling her friends right now?

His mother said no one knew, not even at his old school, but he didn't believe that.

Everyone knew. Hadn't it had been in the Sunday paper just ten months ago, a tiny article tucked way in the back of the local news section? They didn't print his name, didn't describe him, except for three things. First, his age: sixteen. And two other things: his height and weight.

Grady read it two days *After*, in the gray light in his bedroom, lying across his bed because he still couldn't sit up—his ass hurt too much. With the curtains closed against the sun, against any human eye that might try to find him, he held the paper at a tilt to accommodate his mashed-up face, angling the article so he could read it with his right eye, his left eyelid cut and bruised and firmly swollen shut. He read about his height and weight, and the silent, unwritten message of the article became clear: Someone his size should have been able to defend himself, fight his attackers off. Maybe he was only sixteen, but he was a big sixteen, right?

Grady had crawled under the blankets on his bed, pulled them over his head, made his mind go blank. He didn't move for hours. His parents, their faces haggard, tried to act like they always did, that everything was okay, would be okay. But Grady could taste the shame and confusion that oozed off their bodies like a bad smell. They arranged their faces into Good Parent expressions, but their approach toward him was hesitant, uncertain, full of a new doubt. Yes, their Good Parent smiles said, they would always love him. But their eyes told him another truth as well: They wanted to run away, leave him as far behind as possible.

So when they brought ice packs for his face, fed him aspirin and antibiotics, he didn't try even once to talk about what had happened. When *they* tried to talk, awkward and ungainly in their words, he understood that they really didn't want to talk at all. So he pretended to fall asleep, it was just easier.

That Monday, obviously in no shape to go back to school, he stayed home. His mother offered to stay with him, but he mumbled *No*, and she looked relieved. Guilty, but relieved. That was okay, though, he wanted to be alone. He wanted to forget about his parents, forget about himself, forget about what had happened. He wanted to not move.

As soon as they left, he went into the bathroom. Taking hold of his mother's tiny manicure scissors, he carefully, bit by bit, hacked off his hair till he was almost bald.

Then he went back to bed to finish not moving.

He didn't return to school. What could his parents do, drag him there by the ankles? He didn't talk to his friends, didn't answer phone calls, didn't read, didn't sit at his computer, didn't watch television or listen to music. He stayed in bed, wrapping himself in silence.

His stomach seized up whenever he approached the kitchen, remembering what *they* had put in his mouth, made him do, so when his parents weren't home to bring him food, he simply didn't eat. Lying in a ball under the blankets was better than thinking, better than feeling. Better than knowing that what had happened to him had been his fault, he'd asked for it.

What had the cop said that night—the *Night Of*—when he leaned into the back of the car? The car belonging to the woman who had found Grady sprawled in the dark beside the road, crying and bleeding, his wrists tied behind his back, his shirt open, his underwear and pants somewhere down around his ankles. The woman who had called the cops on her cell phone, then produced a pocketknife and cut the rope off, helping him get dressed, insisting he get in her car. What had the cop said when Grady whispered what had happened?

"What, to a big guy like you?" The disbelief in his face, the skepticism in his raised eyebrows, mocked Grady. Then, his voice cynical, the cop said, "Sure you didn't just have a fight with one of your boyfriends?"

Boyfriends? The two men who had jumped him, beaten him, shoved him in the back of a van and hurt him so badly he had screamed, then dumped him alongside the road?

Grady sat still, stunned into silence, his underwear sticky with blood. Boyfriend? Hadn't he been working on a girlfriend? Or had he fooled himself? What had he been working on?

The cop had driven him to the hospital, speaking some kind of code into his radio, then clarifying in English, "Some guy who claims he was raped."

Raped.

Grady sucked in his breath, took in that word. It was a word for girls, not for guys. Certainly not for men. The cop didn't know Grady was a minor, hadn't even asked, assumed he was an adult. Grady looked like he had always looked. Big. Strong enough to take care of himself.

Raped. The word circulated through his brain. He bit his lip to remain silent.

Grady wanted his parents, didn't want them. He fought tears, entirely confused, entirely guilty.

Over the next several weeks, his mother had insisted that he needed to go back to school, he needed to get into counseling, he wasn't eating enough, he was getting sick, she was frightened. But Grady refused, refused it all.

Oh, he let his mother drag him out of bed and take him to counseling once, to a group for adolescent boys who had been sexually assaulted. He found himself in a room with a female therapist and two guys, but they were just *kids*. They were little, looked only around thirteen or fourteen. They were young, they were afraid, they were frightened of *him*. He was too big, maybe they thought he would hurt them. And maybe he really would hurt them. He didn't know, he felt sick, his stomach turned to acid. He got up, left.

As for going back to school, hadn't everyone figured it out? Hadn't his friends wondered why he had disappeared off the face of the earth, didn't return their phone calls or email, didn't answer the door, refused to talk to them? They weren't stupid. They'd start searching and eventually they'd find the article. The paper might just as well have printed his name and address.

His mother finally told Ted that there had been a death in the family, that Grady had taken it badly, was having some problems, couldn't go to school or see any of his friends for a while. In short, that he'd gone *mental*. Had Ted really bought that? Had Christian or Mikey-Mike or Clara-bell, or Tracy? Or had they all finally realized what had happened, realized their friend was—what? Take your choice: weakling, coward, pervert.

Maybe they thought he was gay, had wanted it. But who would want to be beaten up and hurt like that, *forced*? But that's what the cop had thought. Assumed.

Maybe that's what his parents thought.

Lying in bed, Grady would feel all the air leave his lungs. He'd never told them about Trevor. There was nothing to tell. But—

He'd also never told them about Mr. Howell, the man who used to live down the street with his wife and two kids, who helped Grady's father put in a new kitchen floor when Grady was nine. Grady remembered the way Mr. Howell had looked at him, remembered especially the way he'd come barreling around the kitchen corner one day, colliding with Grady. The way he'd grabbed and held him, quickly slipping his hand down to his crotch, groping him, *feeling*. Grady, shocked, had stood frozen, time stopping, the feel of the man's hand on his genitals a thrilling yet sickening heat, until the sound of his father rounding the same corner made Mr. Howell step away, made Grady turn and run to his room.

Why hadn't he run sooner? Why hadn't he told his parents? Did that mean something? It must. Why else would—

Lying in bed, he made himself stop, go back to not thinking.

His mother, standing in the doorway to his bedroom, fighting back tears of her own, said yes, something bad had happened, but he needed to get on with his life. When he failed to respond, refused to get out of bed, she tightened her mouth, turned away, and started humming one of her anxiety songs. Did she honestly think he couldn't tell how she really felt?

How his father really felt?

Ashamed. Helpless. All their expectations about him changed overnight. And dirty. Grady could tell they felt as unclean as if they themselves had been violated.

They felt as dirty as he did.

The cafeteria noise surged and Grady ran his tongue over his lips. They were dry and cracked. Some guy yelled it was time to *pa-r-r-ty*.

He forced himself to look down at his book. Where was he? It was the first day of school, he was at lunch, he had been reading, right? He stared at a word in front of him, couldn't read it, made himself study it until his eyes started to water. *Manifest*. That was it. A good, ordinary word. An okay word. He looked at the next one. *Destiny*. Two words that helped define America. This was easy, really. This word, that word. His finger stroked the paper. This page. He turned it over. That page. But his fingers started flipping the pages too fast, he wasn't reading, wasn't trying to read.

Closing his eyes, he inhaled, then let the breath go. His lungs plaintively asked for more. Well, of course, lungs had to eat, too, it was one meal Grady couldn't refuse. He felt tension skitter away from his shoulders, run down his arms, felt his throat almost relax.

Manifest destiny—the definition of America. Maybe Grady West had a definition, too. Maybe Mr. Howell had been the first to understand it.

SIX

Finally. He'd made it to the last period of his first day at school.

Grady sat down alone at a table at the back of the room. Long enough and wide enough to handle three working artists on each side, the table was pleasantly empty. In the center sat a still life— a vase with flowers, surrounded by an artistic arrangement of rocks and fruit. Would he have to draw *that*? What he really wanted to do was put his head down on the table and sleep, never wake up.

"Damn, look who it is. My one and only true white friend."

Turning quickly, Grady almost slid off the stool he was sitting on. He watched Jess take the stool one down from his, slap his black-and-white composition book on the table, and look around the room.

Was this kid following him? Grady studied the still life. Stick-figure flowers, smiley-face fruit. He could do it. Draw it and get a grade.

He snuck a look at Jess.

The class was supposed to be made up of kids from different grades, with different abilities. The last art class he'd taken had been in the eighth grade; he'd liked it okay but not a lot. He wasn't any good, but talent wasn't the point. *Hiding* was the point.

He watched Jess drum his fingers on the table, stare at the other kids in the room, sizing them up. Everyone was talking, the room noisier by the minute; class hadn't started yet. Grady knew he should say hi. He *wanted* to say hi. But Jess was looking at everyone but him, and Grady didn't know when to say it. He ran his fingers over the smooth top of the table. Calm as a glassy lake. He willed his fingers to absorb the stillness.

He reached into his shirt pocket, pulled out the pen and pencil stuck there, fingered them. Better. He ran his thumb over the smooth wood of the pencil. The shiny yellow paint that coated it felt thick and comforting. He remembered the fat pencils he'd learned to write with in grade school, their cheerful sturdiness. This pencil felt almost the same. He tried the pen. Colder to the touch, it seemed bare and artificial. He set it down on the table and picked up the pencil again, calmer now.

Perhaps it was too late for *hi*, perhaps he should say something else. He opened his mouth to shape his lips—but around what words? He closed his mouth again.

"Still working on our speech and language skills, I see."

Jess smiled at him, widely. Grady set the pencil down, as if he didn't need it.

Tossing his head back, sending his dreads tumbling, Jess waved his right arm in the air. "Ms. Spencer, over here! Remember me from last year?"

Grady watched the teacher turn to Jess and smile. She was pretty young for a teacher, and pretty good-looking. Her light brown hair stretched halfway down her back. "How could I forget you, Jess?" Ms. Spencer said. Then, her smile turning sly, "Just don't take that as a compliment."

"Aw, shit, I mean shucks, Ms. Spencer. You know you're crazy about me." Jess lifted his eyebrows at her. She shook her head, laughing, then turned back to the kid she'd been talking to.

Jess turned to Grady. "She's okay. She's just so *white* I feel obligated to spread a little color around the room." He sniffed. "So. You busy being the silent artistic-type? You could definitely do the part. Pass for a starving artist, star in your own tiny-budget film noir."

Grady tried to focus on the boy's face, noting that his eyelashes were black and curved.

Jess focused back. "Something wrong?"

Grady felt a small rise of fear, tried to swallow it back down. He shook his head no, looked down at the table. Nothing was wrong.

He cautiously looked back up.

Jess was shaking his head, laughing. "My mama raised me to be a good boy." He played a brief round of table drums. "Well, hell." He looked at Grady. "She *did* leave. I was only ten, so maybe there wasn't enough time for all the lessons to take.

"Get this"—he leaned closer—"she dumps my dad, sets out for a new horizon, and gets exactly *nowhere*. Settles for getting a new husband." He snorted in disgust. "The guy's a total loser, too. But hey, you'll like this part. He's white."

Grady tried to breathe, act normal, reengage his brain with his tongue so he could talk.

"I can see that really rocks *your* nuts. Well, the good news is I don't have to live with them. I can only spend so much time with Mom and Moby Dick, you know? Maybe my dad's idea of Happy Hour is alphabetizing the soup cans, but my mom's ideas suck. She even got herself a white kid, a dingbat foster girl. Talk about trading down, right? At least the kid's good for trolling. When I take her with me to the mall, I get white chicks up my ass." He watched Grady's face. "I can tell you're totally fascinated by all this."

"Um, no." Words, finally. Relieved, Grady let his tongue travel over his lower lip. It had split, during math. He needed to get some Chapstick or something.

"No? You're not fascinated? Gee, thanks so much. And here I am pouring out my black heart to you." Jess laughed. "So much for us all getting along." He shook his head, returned to surveying the room. "Now there's a real Snitch Bitch. The magnificent Gwendolyn." He nodded his head toward a girl with straight, chin-length, tucked-behind-the-ear red hair, sitting two tables away.

"At least she's a senior. Next year she'll be gone, and"—he looked at Grady, smiling—"I'll be a happy man."

Suddenly he stood up. "Hey, Gwen!" he called out, overriding the noise in the room. "Wanna go out with me this weekend, get jiggy?"

Gwendolyn turned toward him and half-laughed, half-sneered. "Oh, right. Like, let's." She turned back to the girl sitting next to her and continued her conversation. Jess sat down again, chuckling. "She all but stuck a knife in me last year. Really. She turned me in. Claimed I was smoking dope on school property. But there was *no evidence*. I mean, I'm clean, man. She's a total suck-up. But really, when you get down to it, she's just like every other damn white chick. They always think we're after their pussy, you know? Like it's Grade A Fancy or something."

The way this guy talked was crazy. Grady glanced at the girl. Maybe Jess was right, though. Maybe white girls did think that way about black guys. He didn't know. How could he know?

Jess was the only black kid in this class.

"See that fat chick over in the corner, sitting by herself with her head down, drawing? She's a junior like us, took this class last year, too. Did the same thing—drew stuff every single second, never talked to anyone. She's got a crazy name. *Pearl*. Her parents must have been smoking some really bad weed the day they came up with that."

Grady looked over in the corner. The girl's long, dark, curly hair tumbled forward over her pad of paper. She was overweight, he could see that, but she didn't exactly look *fat*. Not really. Maybe a little.

He turned back to Jess, who winked, nodded at the Pearl girl. "She's good with a pencil, I'll give her that. Won some kind of prize for a drawing she entered in the countywide art show they have every spring. Art by Pearl, I guess. Nice pearly white art. Well, that's what sells, white folk are the ones buying, they got the money." He sighed, banged out a short solo on the table with his palms.

Grady opened his mouth to say something, didn't know what to say, shut his mouth again.

Yawning, Jess stretched his arms wide, then sat up straight. "You don't ever shut up, do you?" He laughed, scratching his armpit. "You are one strange dude, Grady-man." He rubbed his nose, looking around the room again.

"Okay, art by Jess stinks. What I do is *words*." He thumped his composition book. "Someday I'll sell the movie rights to the real-life scenes from my hard life as a brother, make a pile of green. But till then, art is a great place to relax, sit back, and grab a few credits, don't you think? Or do you?" He studied Grady carefully. "It's kinda hard to tell."

Grady pursed his lips. He did think, of course he did. It was just better not to think about some things.

Grady glanced at his watch. Class should have started ten minutes ago, but everyone, including the teacher, was still yakking away. Grady's head hurt.

"See that guy, the one in the blue shirt sitting with that group of kids? No, dork, at the table over there, by the window. He's a fag, everybody knows it. He got beat up last year. There was a big stink about it, so now he's got this group of kids who follow him around between classes like they're his personal bodyguards or something, who think he's hot stuff just because he's a homo— like he's their pet. Shit. Like anybody cares." Jess belched out loud, glanced at Grady. "Man. Had killer tacos for lunch. I think they put these exploding onions in them or something." He belched again.

Grady had stopped breathing.

Fag.

He stared at the boy, his pulse racing, his face hot. He wanted to throw up. Scream or throw up.

"Anyway, he got jumped after he showed up with some guy at a dance last year. Well, like, *duh*, what did he expect? Brains 101, right? But he's white, so what else. I like to think a *homey* homo would have figured that out ahead of time." Jess cracked his knuckles. "Anyway, this guy's a senior now, so I guess the spring prom will be a big night for him and his boyfriend. They'll probably have to call out the National Guard just to keep his butt safe."

Homo. This guy did what had been done to *him*, right? Did it or had it done. Well, that's what gay guys did, right? One of the things.

The old in and out, fag variety.

Jess's face suddenly grew angry. "Would you *please* shut up and listen? Let a polite boy get a word in edgewise?" He snorted with amusement as Grady bit his lip, remained silent. "You know, you're okay, Grady West, even if you are kind of retarded." He smacked him on the arm, made a surprised face. "Damn, you *are* skinny. What's that you got there, a chicken bone?"

He reached to pinch Grady's arm through the fabric of his long-sleeved shirt, but Grady jerked away. *No one* touched him.

Jess pulled his hand back, showing his palm. "Hey, man. Sorry. But I gotta say that even *I* got more muscle than that, and I can't hit. Tell me, have you considered doing Weight Watchers backward?"

He waited for Grady to say something, beckoning encouragement with his hands. "Okay, no go. This boy just doesn't laugh." He let out a long, weary sigh. "You're just like my daddy. The man's an engineer, got *no* sense of humor." He shook his head, turned back to Grady. "Let's return to our previous subject. School dances. You were paying attention, weren't you?"

Grady blinked. School dances. He nodded.

"Okay, listen up. It's a fact that there's hardly any black kids in this whole damn school. How can anyone expect me to find any compatible black, um, female companionship in such a small gene pool? I have to go out and hustle, forage for sex. It's like I'm an African-American caveman. So I say, screw the fucking dances, I'll just stick to the screwing I'm actually doing, you know?"

Grady didn't know, couldn't even imagine it anymore. His eyes stayed glued to the gay boy's face.

"And get this—okay, this is one more subject back, but listen up, it *relates*. I trust you took notes? About that fag guy—his name is Fred. *Fred*. Whoever thought a queer would have a name like Fred? Maybe Frede*rika*." Jess shook his dreads back, flipping his wrist. "Come the spring prom, I wonder who's gonna lead when they take to the floor to slow dance. That should be something to see, maybe I'll show up." He drummed his fingers on the table. "Know any white chicks who would go with me?"

Grady looked down at the table. *Queer*. He never used to use the words that now percolated freely through his head.

He raised his eyes.

Fred sat steeped in afternoon light from the window, talking to the girl seated next to him. He looked to be of average height, with a decent enough build, not ugly. Wouldn't cause a riot walking down the street, maybe, but he wasn't dog food. Wearing a blue shirt and wire-rim glasses, he had brown hair that looked like he'd forgotten to comb it for about a week. Other than that, nothing about him stood out, not really. He just looked regular, like any other guy. He didn't look dangerous or anything. Didn't look like a—fag.

Fag. What the cop thought he was.

What his parents now feared he was. Well, they did fear that, didn't they? He used to help himself to his father's *Playboys*, pulling them out from the night stand on his father's side of the bed whenever he wanted to, then putting them back. But he hadn't felt like looking at a *Playboy* since the *Night Of*.

His father seemed to watch him through a worried haze, as if he were trying to probe his mind, trying to understand what had happened, but couldn't, simply couldn't, and settled for hoping Grady would become what he used to be.

A regular guy, who one day might actually get laid.

SEVEN

"Okay, everyone, listen up."

Ms. Spencer clapped her hands together for attention, standing in the aisle between the rows of tables. Class was starting—relief flushed the tension out of Grady's muscles. "Before we get going, there's a brief announcement from Gwendolyn. Gwendolyn?"

Grady watched the girl with the chin-length red hair stand up, her short skirt covering slender hips and thighs, and her snug pink tee letting everyone see she had enough equipment topside to please. If she wasn't a Grade A Fancy babe, she was close enough.

She laughed slightly and cleared her throat. "Okay, I've done this gig in all my classes today. I write for the *Jefferson Journal*, the school paper, and we want all you new students to fill out the form we sent you. The coolest new person gets a prize." She let her eyes travel over the class, as if searching for new faces, and Grady tried to make himself shrink. But she caught his eye, raising her brows as if questioning him. He looked down at the table.

"The bitch," Jess muttered.

"Okay," Ms. Spencer said. "Now I want all of you to get a sheet of paper from the cabinet and a stick of charcoal. Since this is the first day of class, I just want you to take it easy, draw the still life on your table. We'll talk about individual projects later this week. Then in a couple of weeks, I'll tell you about something you'll all be working on for your final grade."

Ms. Spencer smiled, as kids stood up and started toward the supply cabinet. Jess slid off his stool and disappeared.

Shit! The cabinet was against the wall behind him, maybe a

dozen feet away. Grady froze as kids streamed by, crowding close. Sliding from his stool, he stood up, then sat back down again, abruptly—dizzy.

"Let's see, your name is—?"

Grady glanced at the teacher, her face far away. Then his head cleared and she was standing next to his table. "Grady." He felt her measure him, as if she was feeling his arm through his shirt sleeve, trying to determine who or what he was. "West."

The other kids were moving back to their seats, sheets of paper in hand. Grady really needed this day to be over. He stuck his hands between his legs.

"Oh, don't mind Bean Pole, Ms. Spencer," Jess said, plopping back down on his stool. "He's a little mental, but harmless."

"Oh?" She watched as Jess slid an extra sheet of drawing paper in front of Grady, dropping a stick of charcoal on top of it.

"See, the school administration has assigned me to look after him. Bean's off-balance, needs help getting around the building, plus he needs coaching on his verbal skills. So they asked me, Special Agent Jess, to help out."

Ms. Spencer lifted her eyebrows, her mouth twisting into a smile. "Special Agent Jess, is it?" She looked at Grady. "Let me know if your agent gets out of hand."

Something fought its way to Grady's lips. He tried to let it surface, but his lips hurt from being dry and cracked. By the time the smile finally broke on his face, Ms. Spencer had walked to the next table.

"Way to go, Grady West." Jess was watching him. "Not only can you now say two words every fifteen minutes, you can smile, too. That's an improvement. I'll put that in my report—the administration will be impressed."

Jess laughed, tossing back his dreads, then bent over his piece of paper. The dreads tumbled forward.

Grady inhaled. He picked up the charcoal, held it between his fingers, stared at the blank sheet.

He was still staring when the bell rang.

"Well, let's see." Jess studied Grady's piece of paper. "I like it. Has a certain, um, *empty* quality to it. You might want to save that and enter it in the countywide spring art show, it might even beat out Pearl. I believe the concept of the Vast Wide Open is just what the artistic types are raving about this year." He looked up at Grady's face, and for just a moment, his own face grew quiet. "You really *are* mental, aren't you?"

Grady flushed, uncomfortable under Jess's gaze. He glanced away, then looked back at Jess's brown face, his almost black eyes, his crazy mop of dreads. Jess didn't move, keeping his dark eyes fixed on Grady's face, as if Grady were the most interesting, what?—*bug* he'd seen in a long time. Jess himself looked so— normal. No one had reason to doubt what he was—the same thing Grady used to be: a regular guy.

He had been, hadn't he? He pictured his father and Mr. Howell lugging a roll of linoleum into the kitchen, Mr. Howell's hands large and beefy.

He looked down at the blank piece of paper, felt the stick of charcoal break between his fingers. Maybe Jess was right: He was mental. Why pretend? Why not admit it?

"Yes," he whispered, not knowing or caring if Jess heard. "Yes."

Grady stood outside the front doors of the school, the weight of his backpack dragging on his shoulders. When he was in the fourth grade, he'd tried to sneak a wiggly puppy home in his backpack. He'd made it exactly halfway across the living room before his mother tapped him on the shoulder and said, laughing, "Don't think so, honcho." He had to return the puppy to their neighbor, where five more pups were busy chewing up the rug.

But he got a hamster out of the deal. His mother drove him to the pet store, where he picked out a golden brown with tiny golden ears. Ted suggested his name: Bad Bud. Bad Bud lived happily for two years, running determinedly in his exercise wheel every night, the squeaky whirl keeping Grady company. Then one Saturday morning, Grady found him stiff and cold in his cage, and ran sobbing to his parents. His mother held him; together they made the funeral arrangements. The entire Group attended the services, and afterward his mother served cake and punch, which Mikey-Mike promptly hurled all over the kitchen floor.

Grady smiled. Something was always exploding out of Mikey-Mike, one end or the other.

Mikey-Mike. Despite the warm air, a cold loneliness settled over Grady's shoulders. He fingered the buttons on his shirt with his right hand. This button. Small, hard, shiny. Calming in its roundness. His fingers slid down to the next one. That button, just the same.

He started across the concrete walk in front of the school. This step, that step.

He reached into his jeans pocket to finger the little map his father had drawn for him. But he didn't need it, he had memorized the way. Left at the front of the school, two long blocks down to Pine Street, left on Pine for one block, then right at Willoughby, walk to the end of the street. Four blocks to the public library.

This step, that step.

Easy.

Other kids, going home, going wherever, passed him on the sidewalk, moving faster. He stuck to the inside of the walk, as far away from the street as possible. Still, he snapped his head around every time a loud car or truck passed. He knew that the van wouldn't return for him. The chances of the same two men finding him again were practically nonexistent, but still . . . .

He'd been glad they'd never been caught. The thought of a trial, and the humiliation it would bring, was unbearable. Unthinkable.

And yet—

What if *target* were so clearly written on his back that someone else found him? The men in the van had certainly read *target,* and that was when Grady, with his adult size and his, well, *maleness,* had no reason to think he was. When Grady was just a guy walking home by himself at night from a school concert. From Tracy's concert.

He'd told the Group he just wanted to enjoy the warm air; the November night was so mild he wore only a long-sleeved shirt. The real reason he didn't ride back with Clara-bell and Mikey-Mike, though, was because he'd just watched Tracy, smiling, accept Christian's offer of a ride, and knew he had lost his chance of ever seeing her look at him that same way.

Why had Christian shown up at the concert? Wasn't he supposed to be busy that night pursuing some other girl? And why did he have to show up that night of all nights, when Tracy sent her beautiful notes all the way to the back of the auditorium? A night when her hair gleamed under the lights like yellow fire? Why had Christian chosen that night to finally notice her, to finally smile at her the way she smiled at him?

Those were questions that Grady tried hard not to ask himself. Those were the questions that made him turn away from his friends, decide to walk home, decide to take the loop down Manchester Avenue, a dark, lonely road.

Those questions, though, paled beside the big one, the one that had tormented him ever since: Why had the men in the van chosen *him*?

Now, after his first day of school at Thomas Jefferson High, as he walked toward the library, the ordinary, sky-blue day moving around him like a picnic he hadn't been invited to, Grady couldn't stop his brain from asking and asking the same things all over again. How had they known he wouldn't fight back? What had they seen about him that said, take *me*?

Did they think he was gay? Were *they*?

He almost tripped over the rubber welcome mat in front of the library. He leaned a moment against the front wall, letting the bricks hold him up.

A car stopped and three young kids scrambled out, two boys and a girl, their mother sitting at the wheel, watching. The kids tore across the front walk to the entrance and disappeared inside. Safe.

Safe.

EIGHT

"Grady?"

Huh? He felt a book smashed open on the table under his forearms, heard the chatter of voices in the background. He was at the public library. He pushed himself upright, wiping a small spill of drool off the side of his mouth. His bottom lip, still split, still hurt. His father stood in front of him.

"Dad."

"Thought our deal was you'd be waiting for me outside."

Grady rubbed his eyes; they felt like grit. "Fell asleep." He made himself smile. "Sorry."

"It's okay."

He watched as his father, tall and broad-shouldered, his gut beginning to expand under his suit, looked around the room, then looked back at Grady.

"Lots of kids here."

"Yes." He started pulling his books and papers together, cramming them into his backpack. He hadn't gotten any homework done, but it was only the first day of school. He realized his father was staring at him. "What?" he asked, pausing, his backpack only half full.

"Oh, nothing." His father looked away, clearly uncomfortable. With his short, light brown, all but crew-cut hair, he almost looked military, all he needed was the uniform. But he wasn't. He managed a company that sold and installed outdoor water systems—swimming pools, fish ponds, underground sprinklers, waterfalls. Things for people with more money than the West family had.

Grady shoved the rest of his stuff into his pack. He and his father didn't talk. That was their deal since the *Night Of.* Their unspoken deal. No talking, no asking questions. That was fine with Grady. He got along okay with his father, always had. His father had never been mean to him, had never been cruel like Mikey-Mike's dad, who called Mike a shithead all the time and slapped him when he got angry.

When he'd realized that Grady was a no-talent in sports, his father hadn't groaned about it, hadn't made Grady feel bad. He merely shrugged, found other things they could do together. They went to car shows a lot, Grady liked anything with a motor and wheels. They worked on a coin collection together, played board games. Painted the house. Took turns mowing the lawn, raking the leaves. Whatever. They just did the stuff that was there to do. His father had never doubted him.

Until now.

But, Grady thought, maybe his clumsiness at sports meant something. Maybe it meant—what? That he would grow up to be a weakling, a sissy? A fag?

He ran his fingers over the top of the library table, then realized his father was watching him, and stopped. Actually, he and his father had never talked about anything much, even *Before.* Well, so what? They weren't going to start talking now.

"You, um—"

"What?"

His father pursed his lips. "It's just . . . well, it's just so long since I've seen you around other kids. I guess I didn't realize how thin you've become. Compared to other kids, I mean." He finished lamely, didn't seem to know what else to say.

"I'm fine! I'm eating!" Why didn't they leave him alone about his stupid weight? He was healthy. All his tests for AIDS had come back negative. His parents should be happy. He was doing what they'd asked: eat and go back to school. Otherwise—they had threatened him with a doctor, maybe even hospitalization.

There was no way he'd go into a hospital ever again, not after the way he'd been treated in the emergency room the *Night Of*, not after all the painful and embarrassing things the doctor and nurse had done to him. Not after all their questions. And especially not after what he'd seen in the doctor's face, in his eyes, what the man didn't quite bother to hide. No way he'd be humiliated like that again, made to feel like a piece of slime the doctor didn't want to touch. No way in hell.

He was eating, he was fine. Why couldn't his father see that?

"Okay, okay." His father glanced away, looking old. Then he shrugged and smiled at Grady, a fake smile. "Well, let's go, then."

Grady followed his father out, trying not to feel the eyes of people looking at him as he passed, assessing him, trying to decide what he was.

A nothing, a sissy.

Target.

The morning, Grady had learned, was the one time Jess didn't have much to say. He spent homeroom quietly, scribbling away in his composition book. He never let Grady see what he wrote.

In the middle of the third week of school, as their homeroom teacher droned on about an upcoming assembly, Grady watched Jess stop and chew the tip of his pen. What was he writing? A dust mote caught Grady's attention as it glittered and glinted in the air. Did Jess write about stuff like that, or black stuff? Was there a difference? What did anyone write about? Where did one subject end and another one begin? Where did anything end and begin?

The memories came, fast and furious.

Grady bounced around in the back of the van, trussed like a pig, a silent shriek in his throat. Where were they taking him? Then the van stopped. The two men climbed into the back and turned on a dim overhead light that threw everything—including their faces, which they didn't bother to conceal—into thick, black shadows. The man who had first asked Grady for directions was pale, thickset and muscular, his thin, dark hair slicked back, stubble on his chin. He wasn't young, wasn't old. He set something hard and small on the floor, just at the edge of Grady's sight. A gun? Smelling of alcohol, he sneered, was the first to touch Grady, teasing him, playing with his hair, his voice soft and laughing. "Nice pussy. What a nice pussy cat we found."

Grady, immobilized in blank terror, felt his mind splinter.

The other man, blond, taller and thinner but also muscled, cut the rope off Grady's ankles, then grabbed the front of his jeans, jerked them open and yanked them down, shoving his underwear down his legs. Cool air touched Grady's skin, his dick shriveling into nothing.

The blond man continued, unbuttoning Grady's shirt, smiling at him cruelly, saying, "It's not like we're gonna *hurt* you." Then he laughed and pulled Grady's T-shirt up, hooking it over his shoulders. He rocked back on his heels, raking his eyes over his handiwork.

The first man, the dark-haired one, leaned forward and ripped the tape off Grady's mouth. Then he ran his fingers down Grady's chest, murmuring in his ear, chuckling. "Don't be frightened, pussy pussy. Don't be scared."

Grady's voice was missing. Freeing his mouth of tape meant nothing. He couldn't make a sound, there was no sound to make.

Both men grappled with Grady's long, muscled body in a kind of slow dance, rearranging him like he was a rag doll until he lay bent over, half on his stomach, half on his side and shoulder, his long legs sprawled behind him, numb and useless. His face, with nowhere to go, pressed sideways on the floor of the van, and his wrists, still bound behind his back, burned from the rope.

His mind was missing.

When the blond man took hold of Grady's ass and shoved himself in—hard, dry, tearing flesh—pain and disbelief roared through Grady's body like a shock wave.

His scream the aftermath.

The dark man jerked his head up by the hair, his breath hot on Grady's face. "What's the matter, honey, don't you like it that way?" Then forced Grady's mouth open.

And so they worked him, both ends, together and one at a time.

Grady couldn't think, couldn't breathe. Calling him *sweetheart, punk, honey bun* in high, mocking voices, their bodies now worked into a sweat, their hands slippery with it, they yelled at him, punched him, called him a sissy, a girl, a fucking faggot, a filthy queer.

And started over. Pinched his nipples until the tears running from his eyes blended with the vomit surging out of his mouth. Slapped him in the face. Kicked him. Told him he was shit, a slime, a pussy, pussies got what they deserved. Finally, triumphant, they shoved him out the back of the van. And drove away, the sound of grinding tires echoing through Grady's empty head.

Empty.

Grady swallowed, trying not to feel dizzy. He searched the room for Jess, saw him leaning over his book, pen moving.

He shut his eyes again, trying to find the blank darkness behind his eyelids, but the light in the room made the blankness orange, too much like having his eyes still open. So he opened them, longing for the dark, quiet emptiness of his bedroom.

Jess paused over his notebook, scratched his head with the tip of his pen, then bent forward again. What was he writing? What was Jess pouring into his notebook, that he would never share with Grady?

What would he, Grady West, write in a notebook? What would he say?

Men weren't supposed to rape men. They did that to *women*. Why had they done it to him?

Grady had never had sex with a girl. He'd wanted to, yet when Ted had urged him to get moving, *do it*, he hadn't. Why? Why had touching a girl, the one time he'd actually done it, made him throw up?

He'd given himself up to the two men in the van as easily as a soft marshmallow dissolving in a hot cup of cocoa. As easily as a girl. Is that what he was?

Half the time he didn't even know he had a cock anymore. He felt like it was dead. And the more weight he lost, the deader it became. Sometimes in the mornings, he still woke up with a boner, his hand on the throttle, just like old times. But as he masturbated, still half-asleep, the questions came flooding back, and his erection died in his hand.

Grady made himself look at Jess, his dreads falling forward as he feverishly wrote. Grady ran his fingers over one of his textbooks, feeling its smooth, slightly textured surface. Feeling the tiny cracks. He wondered about the paper in Jess's composition book, if it felt smooth and empty, or if he pressed his ballpoint pen hard when he wrote, leaving tracks.

He left tracks all over Grady, marking out the days for him.

Seeing Jess's head bent over his book, Grady knew the day was just beginning. He had to survive at least six more hours, dump all the questions out of his head.

And when the bell rang, he refused the questions, headed for his first class. Then went to his second. Time passed, another morning in school.

NINE

At lunchtime Grady stopped by his locker to dump some of his books and add others to his backpack. First, though, he ripped off the white envelope addressed to *New Student* that was taped to the door of his locker. Crumbling it up unopened, he dropped it to the floor. He'd seen Gwendolyn and the blond guy she hung around with roaming the halls earlier with envelopes and a roll of tape. When would she give up?

He leaned against the wall, closing his eyes and trying to sleep for three seconds. When he opened them again, he saw Jess headed toward him, toward his locker. A strange happiness washed through his muscles.

"Hey, Bean Pole. How's it going?" Jess opened his locker, peered in, studied its contents. "Practicing your speech skills like I told you? Go ahead, say something, I won't laugh. I'm the one brother you can trust." He scratched his head, continued to peer into his locker. "This is only the third week of school, and I already got enough stuff in here I could sell it, buy drugs. What's your pleasure? Weed? Acid? Meth?"

He looked at Grady, keeping his face serious. "M&Ms?"

Grady felt his own face twist into a smile, saw Jess chuckle and turn back to his locker.

Grady's own locker was fairly neat, just a way station for the books he didn't currently need, plus an extra sweatshirt. He tried to shove another book into his backpack—old and worn, it looked about to split.

Jess squatted down so he could get to the bottom of his

locker. "So go on, Bean Head, *pontificate*. Work on your vocal skills. Speak, O Mighty Mental One." He dragged a book off the bottom, stood up, looked at it in disgust. Geology. He dumped it back in. "Damned if I'm gonna carry that sucker around all afternoon."

Jess rummaged some more in his locker, pulling out a paperback. *Pride and Prejudice*. "Shit, guess I'm stuck with this one." He tried to stick it in the back pocket of his jeans. It didn't fit. He sighed, wedged it under his arm, then studied Grady's face again. "At least your lips don't look like they took a wrong turn down the garbage disposal. You should be able to speak complete sentences by now without bleeding. Go on. Try one out on me. I'm ready." Jess fingered the *Pride and Prejudice* tucked under his arm and waited.

Grady touched his lips with his fingertips. They *were* better. He felt a small pleasure. Maybe he didn't look so awful now. He looked at Jess's mouth—smooth and wide and brown with a tinge of pink—and wondered about complete sentences.

Jess, his face twisting suddenly with anger, turned and slammed his locker shut. "Okay, don't talk, don't say a damned thing. And here I am giving you decent conversation, which is something, I might add, you're in need of, because frankly I don't see nobody else talking to you. But, hey, that's okay. Jess just thought he'd be nice to the crazy. But not anymore. You ain't gonna talk to me, I ain't gonna talk to you. I'm turning in my Nice Brother Badge."

He thumped the open door of Grady's locker loudly, his eyes blazing, and Grady jerked back, his hands stumbling out of his pockets.

Then Jess changed, a windmill on a roof spotting a new direction in the wind. He grinned. "Damn, it's fun to psych you, Grady West. I swear, there's nothing better than giving white people a good work-over." He turned and headed off, laughing. "See you later, Grady-man. Try not to drop dead before art, okay? You look about ready for dissection." He strode down the hall, dreads stirring.

Grady found an isolated table in the cafeteria, tried to eat a piece of his sandwich. Even though his mother had cut it into the tiny pieces he could handle, he couldn't handle it.

Some days he saw Jess across the room, talking to that same black chick, the one with the high looped curls tinged with blonde, although sometimes she wore her hair down, smooth and curved under. Jess had told him her name—Darla. She was small and pretty, he could see why Jess liked her.

He also knew he hadn't slept with her. "Well," Jess had said one day, sniffing, as they both drew a pathetic rendition of the purple cabbage and orange carrots sitting in the middle of their table, "let's just say the booty train has not arrived. But one can hope. I mean, shit. It's gotta pull into the station some day, right?"

Did that mean he hadn't slept with anyone?

Today he didn't see Jess, didn't see Darla.

He did see the blond guy Gwendolyn hung out with. Bruce. According to Jess, they were doing it. "Contrary to what you may think, O Son of Silence, I am not the only guy who talks. Bruce talks. Boy, does he talk. We're in video production together and he *talks*. If Gwendolyn knew how much he talked, she'd shit a cow." He smiled. "Damn, that makes me happy."

Grady stopped looking around the cafeteria. He slid a CD into his player, choosing Bill Monroe and the Bluegrass Boys. He'd started to bring in his music, the new music he'd found one day on a tiny station on the radio. After the *Night Of*, his ears had changed somehow. He couldn't listen to rock or hip-hop anymore, just like he couldn't watch TV.

But one day, fooling around with his radio, when he longed for something besides silence to fill his ears, to quiet the questions in his head, he'd come across a strangely sweet-and-sour music spilling out of the dial. He realized it was bluegrass; he'd heard a little of it before, had thought it shrill and hokey, goofy hillbilly stuff. But now, as these unfamiliar tunes filled his ears, he discovered a music that let him travel away from himself, become something other than nothing.

So now, despite the noise in the cafeteria, with his eyes shut and his headphones on, each day he listened to a different voice, strayed into a different landscape. Sometimes he followed a path across a field draped in mist, or walked beside a river, mourning the girl he had murdered, pretty Polly. Other days he sat in a cabin in the Blue Ridge, or wept over Joe, the dying brother he couldn't leave behind on the Civil War battlefield. Sometimes he listened to the wail of an old locomotive, the sad stories it told. Another day, feeling hopeful, he walked Nellie home.

Today he saw the blue moon rise over Kentucky, and wanted to lie beneath it forever, let tears run down his face over lost love. He wanted to never move.

The gravelly voices of old men, the lighter voices of young men, pushing their vocals into impossibly high harmonies, held Grady. Women sang, too, and Grady liked them as well, but mostly it was men singing, and they were the ones he listened to especially. He listened as men picked out stories, happy and sad ones, on banjos, pushing against the melody with the shrill singing of fiddles, the quick licks of a mandolin. For the half hour of his lunch, he listened. And these men, who sometimes sang of joy, but mostly sang of cheating and broken hearts, of loneliness and pain, allowed him to walk a new landscape. For the duration of each song, just like them, he started over. Listening, he was a different boy.

In art, everyone had finally decided on their personal in-class projects. With a raspy, halting voice, Grady told Ms. Spencer that he would just continue drawing the still life she placed on their table every day. He couldn't think of anything else to do: His work was terrible, nothing looked like it was supposed to.

A more challenging project would have required him to get up, travel to the storage cabinet with the other kids, bump against them, say *Excuse me* or *Are you working in clay, too* or *Hi, my name's Grady*.

Things he couldn't do.

Each day Jess got a sheet of paper for him and handed him a piece of charcoal. Did it silently, as if this were part of an agreement. Grady let Jess talk his ear off, laying down a new patch of verbal asphalt before Grady even realized the first patch was finished. In return, Jess let Grady sit still, not move.

For his project, Jess had decided to reillustrate *Where the Wild Things Are*.

"It's about time it got a makeover, don't you think?" Jess leaned his chin on his palm, batting his eyes at Ms. Spencer.

"Ah," Ms. Spencer began—but Jess sat up, cocked his head, held up his hand.

"I see my version as a black kind of thing."

"*Black* kind of thing?" Ms. Spencer shook her head, laughing. "Jess, you are the biggest con artist I know."

"See?" said Jess, triumphant. "Con *artist*. You've got me pegged, Ms. Spencer." He smiled ingratiatingly, his dark eyes gleaming.

She glanced at Grady, then looked back at Jess. "Just make sure your *black* thing shows up in your work. Don't give me some lousy rip-off of Sendak that any *non*-black could do."

"Damn. You sure are hard on a brother, Ms. Spencer."

"That's my job, Jess. And watch your language."

Ms. Spencer moved on, stopping at each table to see what everyone was doing.

"Shit, man," Jess said. "Dissing me in public like that. Like black people gotta talk just *so*, to prove they're not black or something."

Grady watched Ms. Spencer talk to Pearl, the girl who kept her head down over a piece of paper all the time. He wondered about the girl's skin, it looked soft. She wasn't fat, not really. But she wasn't thin, either. You could touch her for a while and not feel a bone.

Wait a minute. What was he thinking? He turned back to Jess, hands shaking.

"I read *Where the Wild Things Are*—okay, had it read to me—at least a hundred thousand times when I was a kid. I mean, I spent half my childhood at the library, having stories crammed down my ears. But shit, my mother was going after the white dudes even then—there isn't a single African American in Sendak's book." Jess rubbed his nose. "Just where *are* the Wild Things, anyway? Africa, of course. It's obvious Max should have been black. Mr. Sendak denied me my heritage. I'm taking it back."

Grady made himself not look at the Pearl girl, made himself focus on Jess. He knew the story, knew about Max, who was bad and sent to bed without any supper. Knew about his journey to the Wild Things, the wild rumpus, the supper waiting for him when he got home. He'd read the book—had it read to him—a hundred thousand times himself as a kid.

Grady felt the raspy stick of charcoal between his fingers. Today the still life was a basket containing some sticks and leaves, an apple, a green banana, and several pieces of orange peel. Jess had eaten the orange.

Grady began to draw. Everything was normal.

A week later, everything changed.

TEN

"Okay, everybody, listen up." Ms. Spencer clapped her hands together for attention, and the jumble of voices in the room reluctantly began to quiet. "Today we're going to start preliminary work on your final project." She grinned, and Grady sat up straighter, alarm tightening his body. It was never good news when a teacher grinned. Other students obviously agreed, because their voices surged again, sounding protest.

He glanced at Jess, who had on his best pissed expression. "Shoot," he muttered. "Final project? I'm just getting started with the Wild Things."

Grady ran the fingers of his right hand lightly over the table surface. He lowered his hand to his lap, running his fingers over the jeans covering his thigh—cotton, but rough, not exactly pleasant. Still, it helped calm him. He glanced up, caught Jess, eyebrows raised, watching him. He let his hand go limp.

Ms. Spencer called again for quiet. Maybe the final project would be simple. Maybe he could just draw more still lifes. Or maybe he could draw a colossal doodle. He'd gotten through eighth grade art that way, folding a giant piece of paper into squares and working on it a section at a time, filling the entire sheet with an amazing ballpoint-pen doodle that had even impressed the teacher, though he'd only given him a C. It was still in his closet somewhere, folded up.

"Silence," Ms. Spencer exclaimed, "*now!*" Everybody hushed. Ms. Spencer obviously loved being a teacher. She was nice, she was young enough, she looked good in a short skirt, but she was the CEO of this particular organization, and everybody knew it.

"This project will take a while, that's why I'm giving it to you so early." She walked the length of the room, approaching the table where Jess and Grady sat by themselves, paused briefly, then turned to walk back.

"What I want is a self-portrait. You can work in any medium. Clay, acrylics, oil, watercolor, pastels, torn-up newspapers, whatever." She kept walking through the room as everyone watched. Grady saw how some of the guys darted these *looks* at her, as if they wished they could grab hold of her hair as she walked by, pull her close and run their hands and fingers over her breasts. He knew about those looks, because, well, he used to have those kinds of thoughts himself, didn't he? Back when he was what he used to be.

He felt both relief and a vague disappointment about the final project. A self-portrait wasn't so bad. He could look at himself in a mirror, draw a stick figure.

Ms. Spencer stopped walking, stood in the center of the room, and smiled. "But this self-portrait will be slightly different. It will be a *combined* self-portrait of two people. One image, but reflecting the life and experiences of two people. What they would look like if they were, in fact, one person, and had lived joined lives."

Huh? Grady rushed his eyes toward Jess; in return, Jess lifted his eyebrows, gave Grady a look that said, Well, whadja know— Dumb White Person Idea #5,000,000,446.

"Now I want you all to stand up and move to the sides of the room. Go on. Everybody get up, move. I'm going to assign you new seats with your co-person, then I want you to sit with that person for the rest of the semester, getting to know him or her."

Amid the scraping of stools and the loud moans emanating from a class of suddenly miserable students, Grady sat still. Didn't move. Couldn't move. He felt Jess stand up next to him. Felt him poke his arm, poke it again, then, when Grady didn't respond, smack it.

"Come on, man," Jess hissed. "You're gonna look like a frickin' retard if you don't move. Get up! Sometimes you just gotta do what the Man says, suck it up."

But shoving his hands between his thighs, Grady continued to sit a rigid attention, immobilized. Separate from Jess, sit with a new person, *talk*?

But somehow he found himself standing up, moving. Feeling several sharp jabs in his arm, he realized Jess was stabbing him with the eraser end of a pencil, using it like a cattle prod. He ended up on the side of the room with Jess standing next to him, arms crossed, pencil upright in his hand.

"Okay, now. I've made arbitrary assignments. I haven't matched you up for any particular reason, so don't go *Freud* on me, all right?" Ms. Spencer looked at the students huddled against the wall and smiled, satisfied with the misery she had created. "I mean, the only matching I did was that I wanted people who usually *aren't* matched, who don't usually sit together, to sit and work together. As you get to know this new person, or a person you already knew but maybe never said much to, I think you'll find that an interesting 'self-portrait' of the two of you will emerge."

Grady felt an elbow jab his waist, heard Jess's voice, quiet enough to escape Ms. Spencer's ears. "Right. And my name's Miss Fucking Cleopatra."

"Now there's one problem, which some of you may have already realized. There's an uneven number of people in class. That means one pair will have to include a third person." Ms. Spencer ran her eyes up and down the lineup of kids, laughing as several voices called out variations of "Hey, I'll sacrifice, I'll be a third person!"

"No, I'm not accepting volunteers. I've made the decision for you." Ms. Spencer's next words came quickly. "Jess and Grady will stay together, they'll get the third person." She rested her eyes briefly on Grady, flicked them over to Jess, then turned back to the class. "Now, once you're matched up, I want you to spend the rest of this period just talking, getting to know your portrait-partner. Then, by working next to each other every day on your personal projects, and talking *quietly*"—she paused for emphasis— "you'll be able to develop the ideas you need for your joint portrait. Whether you want to meet together outside of class is up to you, it's not required."

At first, Grady felt a wave of incredible relief. He'd still be with Jess, he'd still be safe. But in that brief moment when Ms. Spencer had looked at him, he saw that she felt sorry for him. She'd kept him with his one sort-of friend because she pitied him, he was a nothing. Everyone saw him for what he was—a failure, a guy who wasn't a guy.

He vaguely heard her start calling out names, half-watched her point her hand at the table each pair was to sit at. He finally felt her pause in front of him and Jess, heard her say a name, felt Jess nudge him. He walked blindly back to his table, the same one as before. Was aware that two people sat opposite him, became aware that still another new person sat on the other side of Jess. Their third.

Grady blinked, feeling a rim of sweat on his upper lip. He wiped it off with a shaking hand, and found that he was sitting across the table from—*Jesus*—Gwendolyn and Fred. His heart lurched side-ways in his chest, heat charged his face. He half-listened as Gwen-dolyn jump-started an animated, one-sided conversation with Fred, her portrait partner. Fred, his pale face muddied with anxiety, nodded silently.

Grady looked over Jess's head to their own partner, their third person, and found himself staring into the startled face of the girl who always kept her head down. Pearl. She looked at him like a frightened deer, blushed, then put her head down again quickly.

Jess crossed his arms and sighed, tilted his head slightly

toward Fred and rolled his eyes. Then he glanced at Pearl, shaking his head in disbelief.

"A self-portrait of the three of us, huh? This should be good." Jess leaned toward Grady. "Really, really good." He rubbed his nose, scrunched up his face, and laughed. "A mental, a brother, and a fat chick."

Grady glanced quickly at the girl; she had looked up at Jess's words. He saw an odd mixture of rage and humiliation burn in her eyes, they were an intense blue. Saw that her face, surrounded by a tumble of long, dark brown curls, was nice, even a bit pretty. Then she looked down at the table again.

"Well, I guess we have to get to know each other," Jess said, taking charge. "The teacher has spoken and I'm a good boy, so I'll get us started, conversation-wise." He smiled innocently at Grady. Interlocking his fingers, he flipped his hands over and stretched his arms out full length to crack his knuckles. A pleasant popping ensued.

"So, ah, *Pearl*." Jess waited until she looked at him again, frightened and suspicious.

Grady, pretending not to watch, watched.

"Your folks in the jewelry business?"

The girl's face shifted and she glared at Jess, fear eclipsed by anger. She flicked her eyes up to Grady, glaring at him, too. She had X-ray vision, it burned right through Grady's eyes, it hurt. Grady dropped his gaze, reaching for a button on his shirt. He fingered its smooth, shiny hardness. Its comforting *thereness*. He studied the table, fingering a second button. Who cared if anyone saw him? He was crazy, everybody knew that, Ms. Spencer knew that, now Pearl, with her angry eyes, would know it.

Gwendolyn prattled on, ignoring Fred's silence. Fred—his eyes a light brown behind his wire rims—looked at Grady, locking eyes for just a moment. Then he glanced away, unhappiness peeling off his skin like a scent.

Grady reached for a surface, and found his thighs.

What had Fred seen? In that moment of looking, what had his eyes registered, what data did they now hold about Grady? What did he already know about him? Anything? Everything?

Grady remembered Mr. Howell's hand on his crotch. Why had he touched him? Why *him*?

Target.

ELEVEN

For the next two days, Grady skipped art—a minor criminal activity that gave him a tingle of pleasure. Instead, he went to the library, slept on his face over a book.

On the evening of his second day of life as a felon, he lay stretched out on his bed, waiting for dinner. His curtained room was comfortably dim, almost dark. He never turned the light on anymore. The light that came in from the hallway was enough.

He'd been thinking a lot lately about Bad Bud. Despite his name, he'd been a peaceable sort. He'd only bitten Grady once, and that was because he'd been startled by a loud noise.

Should he get another hamster? He was too old for such a little-kid pet, but it might work anyway. And it would be a charitable act. After all, what happens to hamsters that don't get bought? *Snake snack*. Every hamster needs a home.

Would his mother drive him to the pet shop once more, help him pick out a color and a cage? She'd tolerated Bad Bud, but hadn't loved him. She probably wouldn't love driving her over-grown son to the store, either—standing with him among a bunch of kids, waiting for him to say, "Gimme that one." It had taken him an hour to pick out Bad Bud.

Still, she did do a lot of stuff for him.

Today she'd picked him up a Del McCoury CD on her way home from work. Grady was eager to listen to it, but for now was content with background noises—his mother banging pots and pans in the kitchen of their small house, his father's voice blending in and around the pots.

He'd always gone to Music Masters by himself or with the

Group, but *After*, he couldn't. So when his mother asked him, last July, what he wanted for his birthday, he wrote out a list of the bluegrass bands and singers he wanted. She'd looked at the list in surprise, but was obviously glad to have a productive task, one that might make him happy.

She'd come home from Music Masters looking completely wiped. "I had no idea that a billion rock groups are alive and well and living in America and putting out CDs every single minute. I looked for this stuff for an hour before I realized I was in the wrong section. They need to put up better signs for us old folks." She handed him the plastic bag, said, "Happy birthday, honey," and exited his room, clearly relieved.

Grady heard his father's footsteps coming down the hall and sat up slowly. He knew it was crazy to have to eat in his bedroom. It wasn't like he was sick in bed. But eating in the kitchen or dining room with his parents was simply too hard. *Eating* was too hard.

His father carried in a tray. "Just warning you," he said, smiling. "Your mother's decided to change her hair again. She's got an appointment tomorrow night." He placed Grady's dinner on the TV tray and Grady laughed, shaking his head. Mom and her hairdos.

Just before he exited, his father paused. "Want the light on?" He always asked, Grady always said no. It was easier to eat in the dim light. Easier for him, harder for his father. He wanted his old son back.

"Thanks for bringing my food."

"No problem." His father gave him a half-smile, a worried smile, then turned and left. Grady looked at his tray. He didn't know how to make his father feel better.

His plate was too big, contained too much food. A chicken breast, mashed potatoes, carrots. A buttered roll. A piece of chocolate cake on the side. A glass of milk. His mother would make him a milk shake later, as she did every night. He ran his fingers around the rim of his plate. Hard, ceramic, smooth, warmed by the food it held. He touched the handle of his fork—stainless steel. Also hard, but cold, unyielding. Depression wrapped its dark wings around his shoulders. It was time to work on food.

For a while, thinking it might help, he had given up meat, eating just vegetables, but even they had turned on him. After all, if the purpose of life is to be alive, then nothing living wants to be destroyed, not even vegetables. Something as ordinary as corn growing in a field seeks sunlight, after all, not darkness. It wants to live, even if on the simplest, most unthinking terms. That has to be respected. Right?

And besides, nothing green and growing ever hunted someone down on a dark, lonely road, forced things that hadn't been invited into his mouth.

Defeated, Grady had gone back to meat.

Now he cut the carrots up into little tiny pieces, cut the chicken into little tiny chunks, and stuck a tiny bite in his mouth. He reached to insert the Del McCoury into his CD player, and closed his eyes. McCoury's voice—high, melodic in a way that pitched a tense energy against melancholy—spilled into the room.

He found that if he chewed each cube of meat as long as possible, until it was the consistency of liquid, sometimes it disappeared down his throat without a quarrel. Trouble is, the longer he chewed, the more he thought of what he was chewing—flesh.

Human flesh—human *skin*—repulsed him now, it just did. He couldn't stand the thought of anyone touching him. Touching someone else was out of the question. On the other hand, he sometimes remembered—when he woke up in the middle of the night remembering—the girl at that party who'd stripped down and parked her breasts in his hands. They'd felt incredibly soft and warm, just as he had imagined—but also deeply ripe, cool and firm at the same time. In those few moments, he learned a whole new vocabulary of touch.

He didn't enjoy remembering her smell, though—mostly beer. It was possible, though, that someone else would smell better.

Sometimes, other thoughts about skin came to him when he woke up in the middle of the night. Thoughts of a knife plunged into the belly of a dark-haired man, then rammed into the gut of a blond-headed man—

He'd bleed them, silence them; peel the flesh off their bones like the rind off an orange, like the skin off a grape. And his victory would taste as sweet as the grape's own hidden, inner flesh.

He'd tie their cocks to a fence post, leave them for the birds.

Grady would lie awake in his dark room, his body rigid, his eyes brimming with the image of a blue sky filled with hungry, searching birds, until reason tapped him on the shoulder once again. No one had the right to murder at will, no matter what had happened to him. How could he, Grady West, ever take a knife to someone, even to those two men?

And yet.

He wanted them dead.

This breath, in—for quiet, for rationality. That breath, out—but for what, really? Why hadn't they just killed him? It would have been easier.

He'd sit up, stumble his way to the bathroom. Shutting the door, pulling off his sweat-drenched T-shirt and underwear, he'd lean naked against the wall in the dark, his skin chilling and prickling as it started to dry, the cold tiles pressing into his back. He'd stand upright until exhaustion overcame blood, overcame muscles, overcame despair and hatred—and pulled him, finally, back to bed, back to sleep.

"Grady?"

His father stood in the doorway, looking a little uncertain. Grady set his fork down, a chunk of carrot speared on one of its prongs. "Yes?"

Holding a crumpled napkin in one hand, his father cleared his throat. "There's a kid here to see you. A black guy. Says his name's Jess."

This breath, in for calm. That breath, out for quiet, everything for calm and quiet.

"He's got this little girl with him—a white kid. Says she's his sister or something. I didn't quite get it."

What had Jess said? That his mother had left, and something about a foster kid? He looked down at his plate of food. Del McCoury's voice was invisible.

"He said he had to talk to you about a school project. Maybe you should see him, let him come on back."

Impossible.

"No. Just tell him I'm not feeling—"

"Thanks, Mrs. West!" A brown face framed by a mop of dreads poked around the edge of the door. Grady's voice died, his lungs deflated.

"Yo, Bean Head. You're a hard dude to find, you know that? I had to all but *wheedle* your address out of the school secretary. Then the odometer on my car just about turned over and died getting here. You live like a thousand miles away from school."

Jess edged the rest of his body into the doorway as Grady's father stepped aside. "Jeez, you keep your room kinda dark, don't you?" He smiled pleasantly at Grady's father. "I parked Charlie with the Mrs. Your wife said I could come on back." He paused, continuing to look up. "You and Grade do all your shopping at the tall-guy store?"

Grady's father, looking slightly confused, murmured something unintelligible.

"See, me and my dad are practically fuck—I mean, fricking midgets. You just about need a microscope to see us. I'm probably as tall as I'm gonna get, this is it." He looked around Grady's darkened room, and made a face. "That's *music*? Sounds like about six cats fighting on the back fence, they all got loose bowels."

Grady's dinner turned colder and more impossible by the minute.

"If you don't mind, Mr. West, me and the Bean need a little privacy right now. We got to talk, figure out how to make our two handsome selves look good in this art project we're doing. Self-portrait of two people, except we got stuck with a third person, a fat chick, and let me tell you, I've been sitting next to her all alone for *two days*, and that's enough." At this, he glared at Grady, his dark eyes practically sparking. Then he turned back to Grady's father. "He tell you about this? I've been trying to teach him some basic social skills, like talking, but frankly, it's been rough. Don't get me wrong, Grade's okay, he just needs to work a little harder on his mouth muscles. Now me, I don't have that particular problem."

Grady's father half-smiled. Stuffing his napkin into his pocket, he looked like he was trying to remember something he was supposed to be doing.

"Jess?" A chunky little white girl, maybe eight or nine years old, with short, curly brown hair, pushed herself between Jess and the door frame. Wearing an ugly puffy pink jacket, she blinked into the dim room at Grady, then looked up at Jess.

The foster kid, had to be. What had he called her? Charlie. This was too much. Too many people and too much. Grady felt sick to his stomach.

"Christ. I thought I left you in the living room. What's up?"

Charlie giggled. "Mrs. West asked me if I want a piece of cake."

"Well, do you?"

She nodded, sending a big grin across the room to Grady.

"Then go for it. And take your jacket off, like I told you to. This ain't Alaska. I got to talk to the Bean alone now, okay?" He looked across the room at Grady's dinner tray, eyed the dark hunk of chocolate cake, then looked at Mr. West. "Got *two* more pieces of that?"

Obviously relieved to have an exit line, Grady's father nodded enthusiastically, said, "Sure, I think so," and turned to leave. Then he stopped, looking at Charlie. "You want to come along? You can have your cake in the living room with me and Mrs. West."

Charlie nodded, smiling shyly, and looked at Jess. "Scram, kid," he said. She followed Grady's father, wiggling her way out of her jacket as she walked.

Grady knew his mother must be turning cartwheels. A little *girl* to play with.

"A glass of milk would be great, too," Jess called out. "Thanks!" He turned to Grady, disgusted. "I have to babysit the brat. Can you believe it?" He shook his head. "It's not like I need any more Caucasians in my life. It's not like I need practice." He snorted. "I already got my bonafides. I mean, walk into my mom's house and it's the Hit Parade of white people. Moby Dick's got enough relatives he could restock the Atlantic Ocean, all of them just *so pleased* to have some genuine African blood in the family. Pul-eeze." He stuck his fingers in his mouth, pretending to gag.

Silent, Grady tried to ease the tension gripping his back. He ran his fingers lightly over the cloth of his bedspread, then remembered Jess's eyes. He moved his hand up to the underside of the TV tray where Jess couldn't see.

"So, O Speechless One, you always eat in the dark like this? Not to mention in your bedroom. Interesting in a way, I guess, if you don't got company. But, surprise, you got company, and I can't see in the dark." Jess reached around the door frame, flipped on the light switch, and walked into the suddenly illuminated room. He studied the little cut-up pieces of carrot and chicken on Grady's plate, frowned, then looked into Grady's blinking, light-dazed eyes. "So what's this, dinner for the Munchkins?"

Grady looked at his plate, at the little chopped-up pieces of food. Well, why not? Tiny servings for a big idiot. Munchkin food, for a giant sissy.

Eat up.

TWELVE

Jess plowed through his wedge of chocolate cake.

"This is the thing, Grade." His tongue forklifted a hunk of icing into his mouth. "If you think I'm going to sit across the table from the Terrible Two all by myself for the whole fucko semester, forget it. Fred is probably coveting my very own little black ass as we speak, and Gwendolyn already has her B.A. degree. As in Bitch-a-lot." He sneered, swallowed a gulp of milk. "And our partner, Pearl, has an attitude as big as her rear end."

Jess scraped the last of the icing off his plate. "She smiles about as often as you do, which is never." He finished his milk. "Sad but true, the girl just doesn't have a sense of humor." He eyed Grady's piece of cake. "You eating that?" Grady shook his head no, letting his fingers, out of Jess's line of vision, lightly rub the surface of his thighs. Jess helped himself to the cake.

"So haul your ass into class, okay? You decide you got to have a mental moment, fine, get it out of the way before art. Got that?"

Jess licked frosting off his fingers, downed Grady's glass of milk.

Got it.

That night, Grady lay awake for a long time, unable to sleep. He couldn't help thinking about the Group.

Mikey-Mike. Christian. Clara-bell. Well, all right, Clara—that was her real name. Had she ever caught on to why the guys in the Group had started calling her Clara-bell? Or at least the other guys had; Grady had been too embarrassed at first. They called her that because, after seventh grade, she'd sprouted these big boobs. Classic breasts, Ted called them. So they teased her, gave her a cow's name.

Well, she probably did know. Clara was the kind of girl who knew everything, including how stupid guys can be. Maybe she thought it was funny. She wasn't self-conscious about the way she looked. She had a good build, knew it, and didn't mind showing it off. She was always ready to laugh at a dirty joke, unlike Tracy, who was shy, got embarrassed, and blushed. So they only told dirty jokes when she wasn't around.

Tracy. Grady made himself flick quickly through his memories of her, then move on. His thoughts of Tracy were ruined now, and not just because of Christian, but because thinking of Tracy always led to thoughts of the *Night Of*, thoughts he wanted to forget.

He squeezed his eyes shut, moving on to Ted.

Ted had given Bad Bud his name. He'd let Grady cry into the phone the Saturday morning Bud died, and hadn't made fun of him or called him a sissy. After the funeral, when Mikey-Mike tossed his cake and punch all over the kitchen floor, Ted ran water in a bucket so Grady's mother could clean up—while the rest of them fled to the living room, shrieking and laughing and groaning.

Ted was a little bit like Jess—fearless. In different ways, maybe, but fearless. Ted had girls, Jess had attitude. Jess, with his nonstop, one-person, verbal karate match, was meaner than Ted— his words could hurt. Ted managed to make everyone feel good about themselves, even the girls he oh-so-gently dumped.

But Jess was probably smarter than Ted. Ted wasn't a dummy, but Jess had a way of knowing just exactly how to overturn your apple cart, before you'd even figured out you had one. Grady wondered if Ted even knew about apple carts, the underlying thoughts and feelings a person might be pulling around with him, like so many apples in a wagon.

And Jess was funnier.

Lying stretched out in the dark, not sleeping, Grady thought of another difference between them. After the *Night Of*, Ted had understood, finally, to stay away from Grady's house, away from Grady. Permanently. Whatever his feelings about it, Ted had finally accepted Grady's unspoken terms of separation. He'd left him alone. Would Jess have been so compliant? Or would he, after being turned away, simply have come back when Grady's parents weren't home, forced a window, climbed in, helped himself to whatever was in the refrigerator, then planted himself in front of Grady, saying, "So what's the deal, Bean Head?"

Did he wish Ted had done that?

Grady let his eyes travel across the blank ceiling of his dark room. How could he wish that? There was no way he could ever have told Ted about the *Night Of*, about what had happened. Ted, the girl-catcher? He would never have understood.

Grady shut his eyes. Men were supposed to fight back; it was encoded in their genes or something, that's what testosterone was all about. Right? Fighting and sex.

It was good that Ted had stayed away. Grady would only have had to view disgust in one more person's face. And disgust from Ted—from any one of the Group . . . . It was better that Ted didn't know, that no one knew. His own private deal.

Grady tried to quicken his pace, but he still trudged down the hall, this step, that step, as if he had weights tied to his ankles. He'd never quite fallen asleep after Jess's visit. Slightly dizzy, he glanced at his watch. Two and a half minutes left to get to English.

Not that he'd read his assignment, the next couple of chapters of *Silas Marner*. He couldn't focus, his brain worked about as well as a computer with the plug pulled.

Computer. He had one at home, hadn't sat in front of it since *Before*. Because—well, just because. Grady quickly deleted all thoughts concerning his computer, tried to download what he remembered about *Silas Marner*. Zilch. But his English teacher wouldn't call on him, anyway. None of his teachers did. Their eyes seemed to jump right past him when they surveyed the room, looking for a victim. As if he were invisible.

Still, he felt the shape of *Silas Marner* in his hand. Tonight he would really concentrate, read the stupid book, *memorize* it so he could pass a test, and then—

He turned the corner. Closing his eyes, walking blind, he all but slid into a quick, disjointed sleep.

Whap! Grady jerked his eyes open and stepped back, finding himself looking down into the face of a girl. Oh, shit. *Pearl.* She stood in front of an open locker, rubbing her arm, looking both angry and embarrassed.

"Um." He looked at the floor in desperation. Then, mustering his strength, "S-sorry." Her face crimson, she looked up at him, her blue stare focused and intense. Then she turned to study her locker, as if she wanted to crawl inside.

"You're the art class guy."

Grady felt the edge of *Silas Marner* in his hand. He felt dangerously light-headed. What if he fainted? What if he fell on her, using her body as a mattress to break his fall?

The girl seemed to be busy examining the contents of her locker. Was she waiting for a reply to her comment that he was the art class guy?

Trembling, his fingers continued exploring the edge of *Silas Marner*, the side where you open it. Dry and rough. Not pleasant. He ran his fingers over the cover. Smoother, slicker. Better. It was time to move, he'd be late for English.

Yet he stood rooted beside her, as if the two of them were locked into a human diorama: Boy and Girl Standing Next to Locker, Looking Stupid.

He stared at her, her head still turned away. Her hair, dark and curly, fell to her shoulders; she wore some kind of jeans jumper-thing, a white T-shirt underneath. Maybe she was a little fat. She certainly wasn't thin, the arm he had clobbered was thicker than thin, the skin smooth and soft looking, pinkish. Okay, her arm was a lot thicker than thin, but not every girl was magazine material. He looked at her jumper-clad body, her breasts two definite bulges under the denim. She looked—

Jesus! Why was he thinking about how she looked? He blanked his mind, stuffing every thought about her back into the thought closet. His feet remembered how to walk. He swung his foot out to the side to go around her. Easy. He could do this.

"Um," the girl said. He paused; he hadn't even made it past her body yet. To his surprise, he saw that she had a rosebud mouth, one like they paint on dolls. He hadn't noticed that before. A little girl from his neighborhood had had endless dolls with rosebud mouths. Pearl had a mouth like that. He hadn't thought anyone in real life really did, but she did.

Tracy didn't.

Grady reached for a button on his shirt. Smooth, slick. Comforting in its permanent roundness. He slid his hand down to the next one.

"You haven't been in class."

Grady tried to clear his throat, feeling a blush begin to warm his skin. "N-no." When had he become a stutterer?

"Well, you're supposed to be there. We've got this project. The portrait-thing. We're supposed to, you know . . ." Her voice faded to nothing and she looked away.

His face hot, Grady studied the tiles on the floor: light gray with splotches of a darker gray. He looked at his feet, remembered he could walk, and started them up again. *This step*, he was late for English—although really, what did it matter? *That step*, passing her.

"Wait."

Grady froze, fear scrambling up his spine.

"Are you, I mean, are you sick? Or something? You look . . . ." Her voice wobbled, disappeared again.

"No," he murmured. Did she hear him? He didn't know; he willed his feet to continue. This step, really, that's all that was required to make it down the hall. That step. Even idiots could walk. He counted his breaths, this one, in—for survival. That one, out—but for what? Faith. Faith that another breath would follow.

Assuming, that is, you wanted another breath to follow. Grady let his feet pull him down the hall.

THIRTEEN

Grady stared at his Botany quiz. Another D. This grade would definitely bother his mother. But he was passing, wasn't he? Sometimes you had to take the positive approach.

Wearing just his long-sleeved shirt, no jacket or pullover, he sat at a picnic table outside school, freezing. Everyone was standing around or sitting somewhere, at other picnic tables or on the lawn, jacketless and freezing. A girl had hurled big time in the middle of lunch, clearing out the cafeteria in about thirty seconds. Grady found a table next to the Dumpsters.

He wrapped his arms around his chest, conserving heat, and made himself forget about Botany. What about his encounter that morning with Pearl? It was an accidental clobbering. But what if she wanted to *talk* to him now, or something? She was a little odd, he could see that, but she was a girl. And girls—

He needed his music. He slid a CD into his player, positioned the headphones, and listened to Dudley Connell, in his high, urgent tenor, defy the entire world—daring anyone and everyone to talk about himself and his girl, both once wild, now wild with love.

Would Grady ever be like that, brave enough to let the whole world judge him? Not likely. It was pretty much on record that he wasn't brave about anything, wasn't capable of bravery, would let two men—

The headphones popped forward off his head. Shocked, his eyes shot open to find Jess, enveloped in an oversized sweatshirt, standing on the other side of the table, holding the headphones. Jess tugged the body of the CD player across the table, set his black-and-white composition book down and put the headphones on, adjusting them to accommodate his dreads. He listened and rolled his eyes, then pulled the headphones back off.

"You really like this shit, don't you?" He handed them back, picked up the empty CD container and studied the cover. "Bunch of rednecks in suits, huh? Great. Think they got any fans who are brothers?" He sat down, his brown eyes penetrating Grady's, as if trying to scan his mind. Grady strengthened his force field.

Jess peered into Grady's opened but uneaten chocolate Dixie cup, then poked a finger over the edge of the plastic container holding the tiny, cut-up pieces of his untouched sandwich. "What's this, more Munchkin food?" He picked up a chunk, pulling the bread pieces apart. "Ham and cheese, mustard—on whole wheat. Whole wheat?" He eyed Grady. "We talking *health food* Munchkins?" He put the chunk back together, popped it in his mouth and chewed. "Not bad, I guess. If you're into fiber." He took another piece. "So, you showing up this afternoon in art? Just checking."

Grady punched the off button on his player.

Jess worked on the rest of Grady's sandwich, his dark eyes probing him. Then he swung his head to the right. "I got a little lady I got to see sometime before the end of the ice age, so how's about an answer?" He turned back to Grady.

Grady saw Darla standing under a tree talking to another girl, a white chick. Both of them had their arms wrapped tightly around their chests, and were kind of hopping up and down, trying to keep warm. He had a sudden, vivid image of breasts— the way nipples stand up in the cold and salute. *Jesus*. He disengaged his hands from under his bent arms and let his fingers travel the underside of the table. Yuck. He pulled his hands out quickly, hoping what he'd just encountered belonged to the vegetable family.

"I'm waiting."

Go to art class, sit between Jess and Pearl? After this morning, when he'd plowed into her? No.

"Tell you what, Bean Head. You don't show, and Special Agent Jess is gonna bust your ass. Turn you in. That's right." Jess's dark eyes narrowed, taking pleasure in his new scheme, pleased with Grady's alarm.

"You don't show and I'm gonna do it, call in the school authorities. Let's see, they'll get you on, oh, at least three charges." He grinned, whipping his index finger into the air. "Charge #1: Skipping class. Don't look so shocked, Grady-man. I'm only doing my job, maintaining proper school values and all."

He raised his middle finger. "Charge #2: Being an outright mental, who's got this weird obsession with rubbing his fingers all over everything. And that will sound as strange as it really is, buddy-boy. The administration will think they're harboring a frickin' pervert.

"Hey, don't go looking like you're gonna pass out on me, okay? I'm not peeling you up off the ground. You go down and you stay there till you defrost sometime next spring." He glared at Grady, raising his ring finger.

"Listen up, bucko. Charge #3: Eating Munchkin food. They'll nail you for sure on that one. Scream eating disorder, kick your butt out the door to the nearest hospital. I mean, any guy who's as tall as Mount Everest and weighs in at, what, five pounds, tops, any guy who eats his food cut up into little bitty pieces like you do is totally Mental City. It's not like I'm the only one who's noticed you're a little on the svelte side. Several of us have bets on how long you're gonna remain upright. So, okay, usually girls get eating disorders, but gender bending is in these days, you'll be our own little mutant."

Grady tried desperately to show nothing on his face.

"All you have to do is walk into class like a big boy."

Grady lowered his head into his hands.

"Hey, you don't have to cry about it. Look at me, Bean, would you? Okay, you're not a mutant. Strange, yes. Really strange. But that's just what they're looking for on TV these days."

Grady didn't move.

"I could use some eye contact here."

Grady felt the hard flick of Jess's finger, snapped against the side of his face.

"Okay, man. That's the way you want it, I'll leave you to your Happy Hour, your very own mental moment. Don't let me interrupt."

Head still bent, Grady ran his hand over his eyes, then opened them, staring at the top of the picnic table. Shouldn't Jess be about frozen by now? He was wearing only a sweatshirt. He didn't have any body fat to speak of. Shouldn't he go inside and seek out a warm, hurl-free zone? Grady reached for the pencils in his shirt pocket, taking one out and running his fingers quickly up and down its surface. Better. He started on the second pencil.

"Uh, Grady? Bean Pole? Bean Head?"

He stopped.

"I can see this is a special time for you, but—are you coming to class or not?"

Grady set the pencils carefully on the tabletop, already missing their shiny surfaces. What could he say?

Jess studied him, his face sharp and watching. Then his eyes shifted, his face suddenly filled with uncertainty, his eyes radiating a dark anxiety. Grady looked down at his pencils. What was Jess upset about? He'd never seen his real face before. He looked back—it was gone.

Maybe Jess didn't want to talk to Pearl, or sit across from Gwendolyn and Fred, alone. Didn't want to be the only black guy in a room full of honkey-butts. Or—or anything. Maybe he needed somebody with him, even someone as white as Grady. His own private deal.

It took all Grady's strength not to pick up his pencils.

"Okay," he mumbled, finally answering Jess's question. It was only fair. Jess had been there for him every day, getting his piece of paper and charcoal, keeping him safe. *Okay.* This word, easily said. Not a bad word, really. A surrender word. He'd surrendered before. Hadn't he given in to the two men in the van? Hadn't he somehow said to them, silently, *Okay*?

"Okay, what?" Jess reassigned his lips to smile duty, knowing he had won. His black eyes glinting, he pushed Grady once more. "Special Agent Jess needs just a *little* more reassurance."

Grady searched for his voice. "I'll—come." Easy.

"Good." Jess stood up. "You'll come. That's all I wanted to hear. Now I can go defrost." He pushed the still frozen chocolate Dixie cup toward Grady. "You know, you might actually try to eat something once in a while. You get any skinnier and someone's gonna mistake you for a rubber band, snap you right up against somebody's butt. So I'll see you in art, okay?"

Okay.

Grady sat in the toilet stall, his pants scrunched down by his feet. Somehow, he'd made it back into the school, into an empty bathroom. He'd thrown up, flushed, then for some reason lowered his jeans and sat down. He didn't know why. He didn't need to do anything. His penis drooped between his legs like a limp slug.

He sank into darkness, into a kind of sleep. That must be it. He must be asleep and dreaming. He couldn't be awake and remembering, because what he was remembering hadn't happened. It couldn't have.

In what had to be a dream and not a memory, he was alone somewhere in a dark place. Then, he wasn't alone. He felt a warm hand touch his dick, his privates. His pelvis jerked, he tensed, but—*stupid*—he was alone, touching himself, just like every guy did. He was dreaming about his own hand, warm and sticky with sweat, touching his own skin. His own hand wrapping itself around his cock, pulling and squeezing it as it grew larger, became engorged.

The dream became vivid, electrifying.

Inside his head, inside this dream, his hand gripped harder, pulling faster. He stood up, leaning against the side of the stall, his hips rocking slightly with the movement. The shaft grew stiffer, the skin hotter. In this neon dream, he masturbated, his speed and direction absolutely clear as his hand urged him on, desire quickening, now leaping and galloping like a horse toward ecstatic explosion.

Inside his head, inside this crazy dream of sex, he was close, he was at the edge, he hovered right at the cusp—a volcanic pressure, like muscles straining against unbearable weight, pushing him, forcing him. And then it happened, the unbearable explosion of *yes!* screaming and singing through his skin, through his veins, his heart, his penis, his entire body convulsing, laughing and crying with it. The undistilled thrum of the universe coursing through his own flesh, his own center, hurtling him outward into a vast, unending cosmos. The first explosion, the primal big bang. He came, his hand slick with—

Grady stopped, stunned.

Leaning against the side of the stall, his hand sticky, he remembered.

Was it the hand of the dark-haired man or the blond who persuaded him to come, making him believe that then it would be over, that once it was done they'd leave him alone?

It would never be over.

Accomplice. What the paper had suggested. They'd taken him precisely because they could, because he was theirs to take. They'd known it from the beginning. Somehow they'd known.

Target.

FOURTEEN

Grady sat stiffly between Jess and Pearl. Also across from Gwendolyn and Fred. Could they smell him? Did he have *Jerked Off in Public Restroom* emblazoned over his head in neon?

He lightly ran his fingers over his jean-clad thighs, then stopped, remembering that now someone besides Jess might see.

Animosity hung like an bleak fog over the table.

He knew how Gwendolyn and Jess felt about each other—*grrr*. She'd turned him in for smoking dope. And Fred—well, Jess's disdain for Fred was clear.

Jess got up from his stool, reappearing with a sheet of paper for Grady, a piece of charcoal. He piled his own sheets of brightly hued Wild Things paintings in front of him, rummaged through them, and selected one to work on.

To his right, Pearl opened a large pad of drawing paper, turning the pages carefully. Stopping at one, she stared at the drawing on it for a moment, then reached for a dark pencil lying on the table. Grady reached for his own pencils, pulling one out of his shirt pocket, running his fingers quickly up and down its yellow shaft. Smooth—like Pearl's skin.

Oh, wait a minute, hell.

He put it down, tried the second one. Also smooth, but bumpy where the name of the pencil had been stamped into the wood. It was more like Jess, who comforted and hurt at the same time. A Jess pencil.

Oh, double hell! Why was he thinking of Jess?

Flustered, Grady stuck his pencils back in his pocket and looked at Pearl's drawing. A man's face filled the entire page. His skin faintly etched with wrinkles, his chin roughened by stubble, he stared outward, his expression that of someone startled into some kind of painful awareness. He looked as if he had been caught in the act of finally understanding something—and his understanding made him sick with regret. The picture was good. *Really* good. Jess had been right. She could draw.

Pearl turned her head, appraising him with her defiant, X-ray eyes. He quickly turned away, focusing on his blank piece of paper. Picking up the charcoal, trying to act normal, he studied the still life sitting in front of him. It was the usual crummy arrangement, this one containing oranges and a green speckled squash. Ms. Spencer always added a little something different, but it didn't help. Jess had already gotten to the banana. The peel lay sprawled across his black-and-white composition book, shoved by the Wild Things paintings into the center of the table.

Grady wondered again, as he had many times, what Jess wrote about, why he carried the notebook around with him all day. He knew that Jess would never tell him, would never show him what he'd written.

He toyed with the charcoal, not wanting to get started. Waiting, he heard the noise he'd been ignoring: Gwendolyn— talking talking talking, Fred making an occasional response like, "Um." Grady carefully raised his eyes. Her sleek chin-length red hair hooked behind her ears, Gwendolyn was making a collage or something, working with tissue paper and pictures cut out of magazines, chattering as she worked.

"And then, when I was twelve, we moved here, and let me tell you, I was lost! No friends, no nothing. It was summer, so I wasn't even around kids in school or anything. But then my parents joined this pool, so I finally got to meet a couple girls. We all had it *really* bad for one of the lifeguards. He was totally hot."

She crumbled up a wad of tissue paper, painted it down on the thin board in front of her with a watery glue. "You know, we could put something like that in our joint portrait. I mean, me being so hetero and all, and you being gay, both of us maybe liking the same guy. We could do a face with two pairs of eyes, both looking at the same person. That would be total, don't you think?" She continued pasting, oblivious to the quick, exasperated glance Fred cast in her direction.

That's when Grady realized he was looking at Fred. He saw how Fred's eyes darted about, uncertain, patrolling his surroundings, watching. But watching for what? Probably for guys like Jess.

And like himself.

Ashamed, Grady looked away, made himself stop thinking about Fred, stop thinking altogether.

He gazed at the boring still life in front of him, hearing Jess murmur, "Shit, I smeared it. Well, it'll just have to be a *bigger* Wild Thing." Grady glanced back at Fred, wondering what he was really like, what he really did with his boyfriends. Did he—

His face burned. Why did every thought he ever had have to be so stupid? What did he care what Fred did?

He watched, pretending not to watch, as Fred, his mouth drawn into a tight, hard line, finally focused—on Jess. His eyes, not quite hiding the anxiety that laced them, were both defensive and angry.

Grady swallowed.

Then Fred turned to his own project, picking up a chunk of wood on the table in front of him, turning it over in his hands.

Grady watched Jess put the finishing touches on some kind of giant apelike creature. Maybe it was King Kong. It seemed to be holding what looked like a bald, naked Barbie doll in its grip. Jess picked up a smaller brush, giving the doll red hair—a straight, chin-length, tucked-behind-the-ear kind of red hair.

Grady began to sketch Jess's composition book, drawing curvy lines on top of it for the banana skin. He tried to shade things in with the charcoal, rubbing it with his finger to make shadows, but he didn't know how to do it right. All his drawings looked like they had a day-old beard, and this banana skin already needed a shave. He watched Jess paint red pubic hair on the naked Barbie girl, and wondered if he should borrow one of his brushes.

Fred was carving something in the block of wood, whittling or carving something out of it, using some kind of delicate knife or tool; a few other tools lay scattered on the table. Grady couldn't make out what he was carving. Maybe a bird or animal.

"So, I found out you went to Delmont last year. How come you transferred to Jefferson?"

Grady stopped breathing. Gwendolyn stared at him. "I mean, that's kind of unusual, isn't it? I checked, and you still live around Delmont."

She stroked her lips with a magazine picture, her eyes lethal— her guile encircling him like a snake closing in on a rat. Grady could sense her pleasure—*smell* it—and his throat constricted.

Jess intervened. "Still spying on the innocent?" He plunked his brush down. "What the hell were you doing in Grady's records?"

"I wasn't *in* his records. Anyone can find out where anybody lives. And I'm not spying on him." Gwendolyn sneered. "The *Journal* is running a contest."

"Still? I thought that piece of shit was over with by now. So what's the prize? A date with the idiots who thought it up—Gwen and her loyal sidekick, Bruce the Blond Stud?" Grady could feel contempt rising off Jess like steam heat.

Gwendolyn's eyes blazed. "Leave Bruce out of this. Just because *you* got kicked out of journalism last spring." She smirked and turned to Grady. "For smoking dope after school—*in* the class-room."

"He knows the story, *Gwenneth*. And it's totally bogus."

She laughed. "Oh, my." She looked at Grady. "Jess is so glori-ously bright or something he gets to sign up for journalism a year ahead of everybody else. *I* had to wait till my junior year. And then he blows it! Like he was really working on a story about marijuana use by kids at Jefferson!"

"Like you were really doing anything but working on your Snitch Badge." Jess's voice rose. "There was no evidence."

This had happened in journalism class? Jess hadn't mentioned that part. Grady felt surprise. Jess had planned to be on the paper?

"Like *smell* isn't evidence? Listen, someone had to turn you in, and I'll tell you why. Because people like you ruin things for everybody else. The *Journal* would have been shut down in a fast second if you'd succeeded in turning it into a dope rag."

She turned back to Grady. "You really shouldn't let Jess speak for you, you know. He's simply not reliable. So tell me, have you figured out yet what you're putting into your three-way portrait?" She teased him with her eyes. "Any deep, dark secrets?"

Grady lowered his gaze, then glanced at Pearl. She stared at Gwendolyn as if she were a repulsive, flesh-eating, red-headed alien from another planet. Space travel had been conquered, she'd just landed, Earth was doomed.

Sitting next to Gwendolyn, Fred looked confused. This wasn't his war.

But it was Jess's. All the wars were Jess's. He cleared his throat. "I can tell you what we're putting in our portrait." He quietly cracked a knuckle. "See, what I figure is, we got stuck with a three-person portrait to begin with, so why not just go ahead and include everybody here at the table? Be group-portrait *chums*. So this is what we're gonna do. Make a tall, incredibly skinny hermaphrodite out of coat hangers and papier-mâché. It won't have any brains, but it will have a big rear end. We'll give it red hair in honor of you, Gwen. And, while we can only in good conscience give it medium-sized breasts, I can promise you a variety of extra-large dicks." Jess parked his elbows on the table, his voice cold. "So there'll be something for everyone. Tits for the guys, me and Grade. Dicks for the girls—assuming, Gwen, you know what a dick is? And, not to leave out the fag"—he shifted his gaze to Fred—"a Grade A Fancy butt hole."

Silence. It tightened the air like the tension before a storm.

Then Fred was up, moving, his face an explosion of mottled rage—a missile burning heat, seeking target. "You fucking bastard!"

Oh Christ oh Jesus oh shit, he'd kill them, Fred would kill them, he'd beat them and kill them, oh, God, he'd—

Grady stood abruptly, shoving and toppling his stool over on the floor behind him, the loud clatter ringing through the room. Turning blindly, he just managed to clear the knocked-over stool. He couldn't see anymore, he didn't know where he was, he was lost. He heard Jess's voice, as fuzzy and metallic as if it came in over a time warp. "Let *go* of me, you fucking pervert!"

Grady's foot tangled up in something. Tripping, he hit the floor.

FIFTEEN

The entire class was up, screaming and yelling, as Jess and Fred tried to kill each other. Sprawled on the floor, Grady tried to escape, succeeding only in further entangling his foot in the strap of the backpack looped around his ankle.

Pearl, fear bright in her eyes, stopped her own crazy gallop from their table, squatting beside him to yank frantically at the backpack.

Ms. Spencer bounded toward Jess and Fred, shrieking, then backed away as they whirled into the wall. "Stop it! Stop it! Stop it!"

They sprang apart.

Breathing hard, they stood as if suspended in air. Then Jess charged, shoving Fred against the counter. Fred, taller and bulkier but momentarily stunned, had to settle for grabbing the front of Jess's shirt, spinning him around and slamming his back into the wall.

Grabbing unsuccessfully at the wall, Jess slid down, reaching to clutch the edge of the counter. He pulled himself upright, standing awkward and panting for one moment too long, his face open to Fred's fist. Jerking back from the punch, he hit the wall again and half-fell to the floor, but somehow steadied himself. Taking aim, he slammed his shoulder into Fred's gut, sending him flailing backward across the floor.

And directly toward the table where Grady and Pearl were crouched, wrestling with the backpack.

Christ! Combatant arms and legs almost on top of them, Grady scrambled under the table, grabbing Pearl's jumper and yanking her in after him. They blinked at each other.

Ms. Spencer danced in close, Evander Holyfield in a skirt. The sheer force of her presence moved the battle back.

Panting, lightheaded, Grady watched, transfixed. With his size, Fred had the better odds, but Jess hung in. The fight moved with a vengeance back to the counter next to the supply cabinet, Fred clamping Jess's head in an arm lock.

Jess tried unsuccessfully to wrench himself away. Triumph dawned on Fred's face. Shrieking, "I've had it with shitheads like you!" he spun Jess around. Repositioning his body, he tightened his hold and readied himself for the kill.

Jess wiggled furiously. Fred almost lost his grip.

Ms. Spencer bobbed helplessly around the edge of the fight, reduced once more to a spectator. "Stop it! Stop it! Stop it!"

Fred regained his hold and prevailed, positioning himself to finish Jess—slam his head into the wall, make some serious brain pudding, email him straight to hell. But Ms. Spencer finally rallied her troops: A bunch of guys jumped in and pulled them apart.

The class stamped its feet, clapping and cheering as the assailants were subdued. Blood from his nose dribbling all over his face and shirt, Jess looked shocked, stunned into silence. Fred's wire rims were mashed on his face, but he stood flushed with pride. A minute more and he'd have won. Everybody knew it.

Pearl scooted out from under the table and pulled herself to her feet. Embarrassed, Grady followed, abruptly hoisting himself upright.

Blood drained from his head. Dizzy, it was all he could do to remain standing. But he did.

Across the room, Fred and Jess stood apart, yet remained engaged, breathing hard, slick with sweat, glaring at each other.

Astonishment and rage were etched across their faces, as if they had just discovered a new pleasure—mauling flesh, breaking bones, spilling blood—and wanted to do it again. Win or lose, do it again.

Touch, ferociously.

Fight.

The thing Grady couldn't do. The thing he hadn't done one night long ago.

Pearl touched his sleeve. "Are you okay?" she asked, her face wide with anxiety. He nodded, willing the fuzz out of his head, shaking her hand off his arm.

Ms. Spencer stepped between the contenders, her face flushed, her mouth about to open up for business, start a lecture. Then she stopped and looked back at Grady, the rest of the room looking, too.

Grady wanted to disappear.

"He's okay," Pearl said, making her voice loud enough to cross the room. "He just tripped."

The door opened and Mr. Edrickson, the vice-principal, stepped into the room with a security guard.

Ms. Spencer spoke to the two men. The security guard clamped a hand on both Fred and Jess, and the vice-principal walked over to Grady. Pearl stepped back, and for a moment Grady wanted her to stay. He tried not to cringe when Mr. Edrickson asked if he'd been hit by either Jess or Fred in the fight. Grady shook his head no, saying, in a quiet, raspy voice, "I just fell, that's all." Surprising himself that he could put so many words together so quickly.

Mr. Edrickson told him to report to the nurse anyway, he didn't look good, then went back to Jess and Fred. With the security guard's assistance, he hauled them away.

Ms. Spencer ordered everyone back to their tables. As a loud, disappointed moan sounded through the room—the fight was over, darn it!—Ms. Spencer turned to Pearl, still standing awkwardly nearby. "Take him to the nurse, would you? He looks like he's about to pass out."

Grady watched as Pearl, her face pink with embarrassment, nodded.

Pass out? *Take* him to the nurse's office?

Like hell.

SIXTEEN

Trudging down the hall beside Pearl, his backpack slung over one shoulder, Grady wanted to kill Ms. Spencer. How could she have made him look any stupider? Having him hauled off to face the medical authorities by a girl. A *fat* girl!

He glanced down at Pearl's face, her flushed cheeks. She didn't look at him, didn't talk. She probably felt as stupid and embarrassed as he did. Who wanted to be seen escorting a mental to the sickroom?

Grady reached for the buttons on his shirt. It was difficult, trying to feel button surfaces while he walked—this step, that step—trying to keep up with Pearl's fast pace. She pulled ahead, then, realizing she'd lost him, waited at a turn in the hall. She reduced speed, they finished together in front of the nurse's office.

Grady closed his eyes. "You're supposed to go in," she said.

"Okay," he answered, not moving.

She waited, then opened the door. Taking Grady by the arm, she pulled him inside.

Surprised, he didn't pull back. A woman peered at him over her bifocals. This wasn't the cute nurse Jess had once described; this woman had a thick body and gray hair. "Yes," the woman said. "You're Grady West, I've been expecting you." She looked at Pearl. "You can return to class now, dear."

Grady realized Pearl still gripped his arm. He pulled away; she let go. Glancing up at him, she stepped out and shut the door behind her.

The nurse smiled. "I hear you took quite a tumble. You look

pale. Do you need to lie down?" Grady shook his head no, rubbing his arm, still shocked that Pearl had touched him. "Good," the woman said. "Now sit down and tell me how you're feeling, tell me what happened. I've already called your mother, she's coming to pick you up."

"Why?" The word burst out before he could stop it.

"Mr. Edrickson said you fell, were maybe hit in the fight. Or fainted."

Grady's face burned. "I tripped, that's all." His voice sounded like chalk on a blackboard.

"I see. Well, did you have lunch?"

Grady paused, trying to remember. He didn't like the way the nurse was eyeing him, as if getting him here on a post-fight scare had only been an excuse, that she was really trying to figure out how much he weighed. Best to throw her off his trail. "Can I get a Coke or a candy bar somewhere?"

The woman reached into her desk and pulled out a box of Hershey bars, then opened a small refrigerator beside her desk. He bit into the candy and slugged back the Coke like a brewski, like he was a guy in a bar, a regular Joe doing the old chug-a-lug thing. He tried not to belch out loud.

By the time his mother arrived, his stomach, squeezed painfully tight and cramping, felt like it was about to explode, send its contents either up or down. But Grady made himself smile.

He could handle this little problem. Distract attention away from himself. Pretend he was okay.

He peered again at the red numbers on his clock: 1:37. At 11:58 he'd seen the hall light go out, heard his parents go into their bedroom and shut the door—then heard their muffled voices eat up the usual late-night silence. Now the voices were quiet.

Grady listened to his own silence.

That afternoon he'd had to sit patiently as his mother, sporting her new ultrashort, bleached-blonde punk hairdo, told the school nurse, Mrs. Somebody-or-other, that she was afraid Grady had an eating disorder, that he was anorexic or something, that he'd have to go into the hospital. He had to listen to Mrs. Nurse tell his mother to take Grady to a certain Dr. Hawthorne right away, he'd worked with a lot of eating-disordered kids, she'd give her his phone number.

She also said Grady had eaten a candy bar and Coke right in front of her, so maybe with this doctor's help, Grady would be able to pull out of it without anything so drastic as hospitalization; she'd seen other kids do it. She'd start weighing him twice a week in her office before school started, then coordinate things with the doctor. Oh, she said, is he also bulimic?

Bulimic? Anorexic? Jesus.

Lying in bed, Grady tried to absorb the darkness that filled his eyes. He didn't have an eating disorder. He wasn't deliberately trying to rearrange himself, like some dumb girl trying to turn herself from a Pearl into a pretzel stick. He'd known girls like that, everybody did, their bodies going from bones with flesh, to bones with a little flesh, to bones. Ugly. No, what he had was—an eating *situation*. Grady almost laughed out loud. His throat jammed up when he tried to eat, that's all. Call a plumber!

Still, he'd managed to get his entire dinner down, astonishing and pleasing his mother.

He felt the smooth, warm touch of the sheet that covered his body, felt the weight of the blankets above it. Then he reached and felt his stomach. Bloated. After leaving the nurse's office with his mother, he'd stepped into a bathroom, entered a stall, and tossed the whole chocolate-soda mess. It had been ready to exit. He'd just given it the chance it needed.

Now he wondered about the dinner working its way through his digestive system. It had to stay there; he needed to keep his weight stable, distract both his mother and Mrs. Nurse.

He wondered about Jess, about what particular kind of jail he was in: lecture jail, suspension jail, expelled jail. For sure he'd get tagged for his words as much as for his fists—probably more so. Why did he have to go and fight a homo? Didn't he know the kind of trouble he'd get himself in? Didn't he, of all people, know what he'd be accused of?

Grady—at least he kept his words to himself.

Who was he kidding? Since the *Night Of*, his head had been nothing but a talking garbage can. He should be in jail with Jess.

And what about Fred? Grady's stomach, still struggling with his dinner, twisted itself into a painful knot. Fred had done all right. He'd basically won the fight. Jess had used words he shouldn't have, and Fred had taken revenge. Understandable. So— it was okay.

He stared at his clock. 1:59. He wouldn't think about Fred. Thinking about Fred only led to the questions he couldn't answer.

The knot in his stomach finally came undone. Relieved, Grady stretched his hands out, feeling the smoothness of the sheet he lay on. Cottony and warm. Tension slipped from his shoulders, exhaustion finally leaning over his bed, pulling the blankets up under his chin and tucking him in.

He carefully balanced on his stool. The still life—all parts uneaten—sat in front of him. An empty stool separated him from Pearl.

At lunch he'd forced down most of his cut-up Munchkin sandwich, plus a chocolate Dixie cup. But afterward, he'd felt so repulsed he'd had to step into a bathroom and toss it. He wondered if Pearl could smell him, if his smell made her sick.

How would he get his piece of drawing paper? Would Ms. Spencer take pity on him, be his Special Agent Teacher for the day? Doubtful. When he'd walked into the room, she'd looked at him with irritation, as if she was tired of him and his strangeness, his nothingness. His anxiety had escalated. Was everyone else tired of him, too? Would they mock him openly, the way Jess had mocked Fred?

Jess, Gwendolyn had announced triumphantly to him and Pearl, had been suspended for three days. "And," she added, a winner's streak gleaming in her eyes, "when he comes back, he not only has to apologize to Fred, but to the three of us, too! You can bet this whole thing is getting written up in the *Journal!*"

Lecture jail, suspension jail, apology jail.

Gone-away jail.

But it could have been worse for Jess, a lot worse. Fred had thrown the first punch.

With just lecture jail, Fred sat across the room at his and Gwendolyn's reassigned table. With his black eye and a pair of dark, plastic frames obviously left over from an earlier stage of life, he looked broken, as if his initial triumph had leaked out of his body, fast.

Grady, pretending not to look, noticed how some students talked to Fred eagerly and gave him a thumbs-up of support, while others glared. What would they say about *him*, if they knew about the *Night Of*?

He stuck his hands between his legs and watched as Gwendolyn leaned close to Fred, yakking freestyle, no rules, as excited as if *she* had bested Jess in a fist fight.

Grady squeezed his eyes shut, then opened them, refusing to look at Fred again. He made himself concentrate on Pearl as she stared at the table.

Dark, curly hair that touched her shoulders—entry-level babe hair. Navy blue T-shirt etched in white with the face of a wolf. Rosebud mouth. Harsh blue eyes.

A body that would keep your fingers away from her bones for a while.

Jesus. This was crazy. What was he thinking?

He bit his lip, snuck another look at Pearl, then ran his fingers over his jeans. Rough, as it always was. Also soft somehow, like—

"It's poetry."

Huh? Pearl's X-ray eyes bore into him. Confused, he sat at rigid attention as she got up and disappeared behind him.

A piece of paper slid across the table in front of him, Pearl laying a piece of charcoal on top. She waited a moment, standing close to his arm. He could feel her heat, he was burning up. He'd die, he'd suffocate—

She pulled back. "Look at me," she said, gun to prisoner.

He looked, sweat starting to coat his upper lip.

"When you were out those days. Every time Ms. Spencer was on the other side of the room, Jess opened up his book and wrote in it." She spoke quickly, as if her breath would run out before her words did. "So once, when he got up to do something, I reached over and peeked." She leaned close, as if she was sharing a secret that would change the universe, if only he could understand. "In his composition book. He writes poetry."

She waited.

"Um," he said.

"*Poetry*," she said earnestly, as if he simply had to understand, everything depended on it. Grady, his lips dry, *didn't* understand, couldn't speak, had nothing to say.

He could read the defeat in her face, a ship going down. So Grady did something he simply couldn't do, not in the land of *After*.

As she pulled away, he reached and grabbed her arm. Grabbed it, held it, locked himself onto her skin. Realized, shocked, that he didn't know how to let go.

She looked at him in surprise, her mouth opening.

"Okay," he said, his voice harsh and ragged. "Poetry."

"Yes," she said, a smile touching her lips. "*Poetry*. I draw. You get sick. Jess hurts people—and writes poetry."

As if that explained the universe.

"Our portrait," she said.

Grady's hand sprang open.

SEVENTEEN

On his second Jess-gone day, Grady headed for the nurse's office. He didn't dare not show up—his mother had laid down the Mother Law. Climbing aboard the standing scale, he watched as Mrs. Nurse flipped the little metal weights back and forth. He smiled, she smiled. When she turned to write the number down, he gave her the finger.

That night, his mother informed him he had an appointment with the illustrious Dr. Hawthorne in two weeks, she couldn't get one sooner.

Darn.

Grady ran his fingers over his pencils, over his thighs, over the tabletop, but his hands shook uncontrollably. Pearl watched him, her rosebud mouth twisted tight with anxiety.

Okay, he was mental. *Okay?* Was that so hard to understand? He needed *surfaces*.

He started over again with his pencils, with his thighs, with—

Pearl tugged at his shirt sleeve, holding out a pencil of her own—the dark one, the one she drew with.

He took it, running his fingers up and down its roundness. It felt harder somehow than his own pencils, also thicker, the painted coating thinner. A different kind of pencil, its smoothness slightly sticky with the heat from her hand. The heat transferred to his palm, and he felt his fingers begin to relax, his arms and shoulders following. He looked at Pearl uncertainly. She smiled tentatively, so he half-smiled back. Returning her pencil, he picked up his piece of charcoal and turned to the still life: a bowl of apples nestled in a pile of twigs. An uneaten, Jess-missing still life.

He began to draw. Pearl turned to her pad of paper. Grady, pretending not to, looked across the room at Fred.

His wire rims restored, he wore them over a nice purple-and-yellow black eye.

He seemed both farther away and closer at the same time, as if his difference—okay, his homosexuality—were a lightbulb, Grady a stupid moth smacking up against it again and again, trying to understand, not understanding.

Fred, with his fists, was more of a man than he was, right? Despite what he did with his dick.

Girls got raped all the time, but nobody expected them to punch out their assailants. He, though, could have—he'd had the physical strength. Who'd ever said, even once in his whole life, that it was okay for a guy to be a coward? No one. You had to be brave—that's what every book, TV show, computer game, and movie said—because that's how wars got won, how civilizations got saved. And, face it, how chicks got bagged. Victory-making: common, everyday guy stuff, regular work for men—no unemployment, ever.

He made himself turn back to his still life. Wielding the charcoal like a light saber, he pretty much created and destroyed his drawing in one swoop. It looked like a bowl full of bread sticks holding large, misshapen meatballs.

At the end of class, he watched Pearl take his masterpiece up to Ms. Spencer. Pearl's outfit, a rose-colored T-shirt tucked into a black skirt, made her look both heavier and, well—

Grady flushed and tried to stuff his Pearl thoughts back into the thought closet, studying his hands for distraction.

If she looked any way in particular, even if her T-shirt made her look—what he meant was, if it made her breasts look—

His face burned. What was he thinking? He was practically a

girl himself, now—a neuter. He could barely get it up. How she looked was no business of his.

When she returned to the table, giving him a shy, uncertain smile, he ignored her, pretended she wasn't there, didn't look up when she left.

Shouldn't he be out somewhere on a Friday afternoon, getting wild, getting ready to party? Grady sat in the public library, his Botany text under his elbows. Party animal—yep, that's what he was. Booze and babes, both on tap.

Right.

There was no point in listening to his music. Today he had a Doc Watson with him, and Doc Watson—who sang with a soft but steely melodic pain, sounding like a good, tired father singing to his children—always made him feel better. But he knew he'd end up falling asleep anyway, and he'd just mangle his headphones.

He crossed his arms over Botany, lowered his head and let darkness take him. Jess would be back on Monday. Comforted by that thought, Grady sank deeper, letting himself drift into thoughts of Pearl, her rosy T-shirt.

She was real. And she liked him.

What night in a van?

"Hey. Bean Head."

Grady blinked, staring into the gray twilight under his folded arms.

"Excuse me, Avon calling. Anybody home?"

He felt a painful rap on the top of his skull and jerked his head up. On the other side of the table stood Jess.

Jess.

"Man." Jess shook his head, pulled out a chair and sat down.

"You are one bad-looking dude when you wake up, you know that? Got that drool stuff all over your face."

Grady sat up straighter.

Jess tilted his chair back, started to rub his bruise-darkened nose, and stopped abruptly, letting his chair slam forward again. "Damn, it still hurts. I gave *blood* for the heterosexual cause. I'm a frickin' martyr."

He sighed, pulling a handkerchief out of his pocket. "Here, use this."

Grady wiped his face.

"Okay, so I can't hit, that's why I got crunched. But hey, I *tried*." He tapped his fingers on the table.

He turned slightly to look around the room, and Grady, fully awake now, soaked him up, his body washed with a simple pleasure.

Jess turned back to him. "So what's up, Bean? You look like a possum with a bad haircut—like you've been trapped at the top of a tree for three days with a mean dog at the bottom and no barber in sight."

Grady touched his hair. It was definitely time for the clippers.

"Still can't talk, huh?" Jess tilted his chair back again. "Look at you. Drooled-on and mute. Three days away from Special Agent Jess and you fall apart."

Grady swallowed. "Um."

"Hey. A word. Good one, too." Jess let his chair fall forward again.

Grady cleared his throat. "What—" He tried again. "Why—"

"Who what when where why?"

Grady's fingers sought the surface of the table, collided with Botany.

"Still got that voodoo finger stuff going, I see." Jess sighed. "If you're trying, in that oh so plaintive way of yours, to ask what I'm doing here, well, it's a free country, right?"

Grady's fingers settled for a small space between books and papers.

"I've seen you make your way here after school before, Bean Head—I sometimes have stuff to do over this way myself. Even bring Charlie here sometimes on Saturdays when my mother signs me up for big brother duty." He laughed. "So I know where you hang out after school, Grady-man. It's frightening, the way you shoot this library stuff straight up. We got a serious junkie in the making."

Grady smiled, feeling his bottom lip crack open. Wincing, he touched it with his tongue.

"And, just because I got suspended and grounded and yelled at for being the meanest, nastiest brother in the entire universe, that doesn't mean I forgot how to drive. Look, shit happens, you get over it." He sniffed. "Besides, I've been good for three days now. Told Jesus I was sorry. Said my Hail Marys and Hail Freds." He fingered the thin gold chain around his neck. "So how's our little homo doing?"

Oh. Jess wanted information, that's why he was here. Disappointment enclosed Grady like a thin darkness. What had he been thinking—that Jess had come to see *him*?

He reached for a button on his shirt, running his fingers over its tiny smoothness. Chilly, like a small, cool sun, maybe a star—

"Jess to Bean Head. Come in, please."

Grady sighed. So how was Fred? His eye was purple and yellow, giving him that *combat* look, but maybe it was the look to have. Other than that—what did he know?

Nothing.

Except—the color of his eyes. Aside from the bruise, they were a light, luminous brown. And his face—well, everybody noticed good-looking people. He hadn't been blind to Ted. Even Mikey-Mike had had his good days. And so, okay, he'd noticed Fred. But everybody noted stuff like that, that was just regular, wasn't it?

And Jess, with his smooth brown skin and dark, almost black eyes—

Frightened, Grady dropped his gaze.

Mr. Howell had been nice-looking, he remembered that. His mother had even commented once that Mr. Howell was a nice-looking man. But he was a creep, a pervert. As for his hand on Grady's crotch—well, any hand on your crotch might make your privates heat up, right?

Grady tried to quiet his fingers on his jeans. Actually, it had happened a second time—another Saturday spent working on the kitchen. His mother was out shopping, his father had run to the hardware store. Grady could hear Mr. Howell pounding away in the kitchen with a hammer. He'd crept into the dining room to get a book he'd left there, and that's where Mr. Howell found him.

Had he hoped he would?

Mr. Howell reached his hand all the way under Grady's sweats and underwear. Grady, standing still, nauseated but also darkly excited, let him do it. Just let him. So what did that say about him?

Then Mr. Howell placed Grady's hand on *his* dick, shaping his hand with his own, making him rub, and suddenly everything changed. "Stop it!" Grady had shrieked, spinning away. "I'll tell!"

He hadn't. He'd been too afraid he'd get in trouble. But at least Mr. Howell had left him alone after that, and a short time later moved out of the neighborhood, taking his family with him.

Grady squeezed his eyes shut. Okay, he'd been groped. It's not like it was the worst thing that had ever happened to anyone. It's not like he'd been ruined for life.

He opened his eyes.

He could count the girls who had touched his cock, even just through his clothes, on exactly one finger. The drunk party girl.

He could count the men who'd had touched him on three fingers. Face it, the only major sex he'd ever had, had been with men—the two guys in the van. Maybe he'd been forced, but he hadn't fought them off. Maybe that meant something.

Jess, still sitting across from him, still chewing on his fingernail, might as well leave. Grady had nothing to say to him about Fred, except the obvious: He's still gay, you're still acting like a jerk.

Shocked, he looked at Jess—could he read his mind? But Jess remained calm, a kind of impatient patience settled on his face. A kind of irritated acceptance. Grady felt a sudden, strange aching in his chest. Who else knew he was even alive? Who?

He cleared his throat, forcing his voice. "His name is Fred."

Jess crunched his right hand in his left, cracking knuckles. "Got that. Fred the Fag. So how many times do I have to kiss his pink ass to keep his mommy from suing my daddy?"

Grady raised his eyes. "Just—Fred." Then, to his surprise, "N-not fag."

Jess's face shifted, his eyes narrowing. "N-not fag? I see. We got us a sympathizer. Or something."

Grady fought for more words. "Just—not fair." He'd known that all along, why had the word lived in his own head?

Jess's eyes were unreadable. Grady couldn't stand it. He needed Jess, needed his real eyes to see him, know he was there. How could he survive without him?

Unhappiness rolled off Jess like fog off a lake. "I see—it's not *fair*. So the Grady-man takes sides."

"No." Grady pushed words from his throat, it hurt. "I mean—"

"Grady? Is that you?" The girl's voice stopped Grady's heart between one beat and the next.

No.

He made himself look only at Jess, focus only on his profile.

"Hello, *America*," Jess said, looking up. His face, even just the half of it Grady could see, brightened with pleasure. "If you're handing out free samples, I'll take one. I mean, of course I'd prefer to stay loyal to my African-American heritage, but I'm an equal opportunity kind of guy. I'll settle for blond. Ignore the dork on the other side of the table, though. He's got other plans."

Grady made himself look only at Jess, focus only on his profile.

It couldn't be. Please, no.

"Grady?" The voice was tightened with shock, but Grady recognized it. He couldn't not recognize it. "I—I don't believe this. Is it really you? I almost didn't recognize you. I mean, we just about went crazy—." Silence. "Jesus, Grady, *say* something. Are you—is it really you?"

Jess nudged him under the table. "This is your chance to prove you're not a you-know-what, stupid. If I was you, I'd go for it."

Grady stared at the table, his fingers stampeding to his thighs—circling helplessly, doomed.

"Grady. *Please.* Look at me. Say something."

"Yeah, Bean Head. Make like you got an IQ." Jess prodded him under the table again.

Grady squeezed his eyes shut, then opened them.

He looked toward the voice, toward what he dreaded to find.

Tracy.

EIGHTEEN

Jess took over, MC'd the reunion, a DJ working the turntables.

Grady felt Jess poke him under the table with his foot, saw him look at Tracy, heard him say, "So, he's your buddy from way back, huh? You mean he hasn't always been so, um, *mental*?" Jess raised his eyebrows skeptically, all the while rubbing his chin and smiling, switching his dark eyes back and forth between Tracy and Grady.

Tracy stood still, a book tucked under her arm, her face confused and anxious, her light blue eyes darting worriedly between Jess and Grady—as if by not moving, she might understand what was happening. She and Jess did the hi-I'm-me-who-are-you bit, Tracy staring at Grady, finally interrupting her conversation with Jess to ask, her voice tight with disbelief, "Grady, where have you been? What *happened*?"

A question he couldn't answer, for just beyond her head a man turned—

But wait, was her hair really brighter than it had been the last time he'd seen her, the concert lighting making her all but glow? Shinier than that night, almost a year ago, when his life had imploded with violence, and hers had continued on so quietly and sensibly? Even now, though she was obviously distracted and upset, she radiated a shy pleasure. Yes, she told Jess, she did have a boyfriend. She laughed uncertainly at his exclamation of—"Damn! Figures. A black dude just can't get anywhere with a white chick these days"—then turned to Grady, waiting for his answer.

But he didn't have one, for just beyond her head a blond man turned to face him, laughing cruelly. This man owned Grady now, Grady's tongue forever his, forever silenced.

He listened to Tracy, her voice pleading. "We tried everything, nobody would talk to us, not your parents, nobody at school. We just about went crazy. And Ted—" she stopped, struggling not to cry. "Grady, *say* something. What happened? Are you sick, do you—do you have cancer or something? You're so *thin*. And your *hair*—"

He watched Jess study her, assessing her with a practiced stare, then look at Grady with a new interest. He heard Jess's silent echo of her questions, heard the blond-haired man whisper in his ear, "You're shit, you fucking asshole. Shit." Felt the man's hand caress his neck and chest, his stomach. "You're a fucking piece of shit."

Grady felt the edge of a book under his fingers. He needed to say something, deflect Tracy's attention, make her go away. "I'm, uh . . . fine," he croaked, his voice sounding like a hog in a slaughterhouse, its throat slit, choking on its own blood.

He closed his eyes and listened. The library, just behind the muffled edge of people talking, moving about and checking out books, dripped with silence. You just had to be patient, wait for it to manifest—the space between words where no one prodded you, or asked you questions you couldn't possibly answer.

He laid his head down on Botany, and slept.

"Grady?"

He opened his eyes. Jess and Tracy were gone. When had they left? His father stood in front of him, his jacket buttoned tightly over his gut. "Ready?" he asked. His face, pale and lined, looked something like the man pictured in Pearl's art book. Who was that man, anyway? Grady needed to ask. And just where was Pearl right now, what was she doing? He hadn't said goodbye.

He nodded to his father, gathered up his books and papers. Ready.

Grady stared at his plate, overwhelmed by the pungent scent that stung his nose—meatloaf. For some reason his mother had apologized for serving meatloaf for Sunday dinner. Why? Did she think she was supposed to serve a whole animal on the hoof? Some kind of Gutted-Cow Sunday Special?

He squeezed his eyes shut, wishing he could stop eating altogether, ride the black horse of his hunger to the end.

Tomorrow was Apology Day. Just thinking about it made his stomach cramp. He didn't want to sit crammed together with Jess, Mr. Edrickson, Gwendolyn, and Pearl in a small office. He didn't want Jess's apology, anyway, and couldn't imagine Jess keeping a straight face long enough to pass one all the way around the room. But he'd have had practice by then, because first he had a solo performance with Fred. And that one included parents.

His pass out of jail.

He hadn't seen Jess since Friday afternoon in the library. He never saw him over the weekend, but for some reason, he'd thought he might show up, sticking his head around the edge of his bedroom door, saying, "Yo, Bean Head."

That hadn't happened.

He made himself look at his plate of Munchkin food. A slice of meatloaf cut into little tiny meatloaves. A baked potato opened and dissected, cubed—slathered with butter. Peas, Munchkins in their natural form. Plus a glass of milk and two oatmeal cookies—over the stink of the milk, he could smell the sweetness of sugar and cinnamon.

He leaned over, popped an Alison Kraus into his CD player. Her singing and fiddle-playing depressed him sometimes. She always sounded mournful, even when she wasn't. But her music was also soft and kind of wishful, so it wasn't a bad music to eat by.

He studied the dim walls of his room as he chewed, and thought about Jess's composition book, about Pearl's revelation. Jess was definitely not a *thee* and *thou* kind of poet. But probably nobody was anymore. Maybe he was an angry poet. As an African American, there was plenty for him to be angry about, right? Even Grady, as stupid and white as a freshly painted picket fence, could see that.

Maybe he wrote hip-hop stuff, getting set to be famous.

Maybe he slammed in front of a mike.

Whatever his poems were, they seemed to be a secret. He'd be totally burned to find out that Pearl had peeked.

Grady speared a chunk of meatloaf, then unspeared it. The smell made him sick. He tried a potato piece, then picked a raisin out of a cookie and bit. Tiny food for tiny people.

NINETEEN

Grady sat on a metal chair outside the door to Mr. Edrickson's office, his long legs splayed awkwardly in front of him. To his right sat Pearl, looking like an unhappy refugee who'd walked herself across the wrong border. She wore a flannel shirt and jeans, which were appropriate for crossing enemy lines, maybe, but made her thighs and rear end look big enough to land an airplane on. A small airplane.

Grady briefly imagined making just such a landing, then slammed his thought closet shut. Why did he think such stupid things? He was nothing, a skinny batch of zero gravity—who just last night had dreamed of a guy.

His face grew hot as the dream skittered across his memory— Fred's face, as warm as sunlight, his eyes as clear as an autumn sky filled with brown, falling leaves.

Grady had woken in a cold sweat.

So, okay, it had happened, he'd dreamed of a guy. But—he swallowed hard—he hadn't just dreamed about Fred, he'd practically made love to his face. Did that mean, in the Great Monopoly Game of Life, he'd passed Straight, was headed directly for Homo?

He hid his hands under his elbows. What else could it mean? Fred's face had been as clear and intense as if Grady had walked directly into a vivid Technicolor movie, Fred's face the entire feature: subject, star, director, screenwriter, everything. The best, most engrossing film he had ever seen. Fred's face practically sucking Grady's eyeballs right out of his head.

He tried to breathe.

Across from him sat Gwendolyn, endlessly turning a bracelet

on her left wrist with her right hand. With her red hair tucked neatly behind her ears, her slender legs crossed—the top one swinging slightly, her short skirt stretched across her thighs—she looked like she always did: celebrity wannabe.

He ran his fingers just under the edge of his seat, watching as Pearl leaned forward to check the flat, skinny portfolio that held her drawings. Then she leaned back, blowing air out of her lips, and started to peel off her flannel shirt. Grady's fingers lurched in panic from the underside of his chair, but as her shirt exited the shoulder closest to him, he saw that, of course, underneath it she wore something else—a long-sleeved dark green tee.

Snagged half in and half out of flannel, she caught him looking. Embarrassed, Grady sent his fingers back to work the underside of the chair. When he glanced at her again, she was busy studying her thighs, pressing her hands against them as if wishing they would shrink or disappear.

"So how are you, um, you know." Pearl's voice trailed off to nothing. "Doing?"

Grady tried to work his mouth. "Um. Okay." Then, to his surprise, "You?"

Her eyes snuck back to his. "'Kay."

Silence. She looked away, Grady didn't know where to look. Across from them Gwendolyn's foot swung faster. "Yeah," she said, her eyes a cold, sharp knife. "How are you? What's wrong with you, anyway?"

Pearl's eyes swung back to Grady. He held them for a moment with his own, then stared at his knees. Discovering his fingers had escaped the underside of the chair, he sent them galloping back. This breath, in—

"He's fine," said Pearl.

Gwendolyn rolled her eyes and smirked. "Right." She refocused on Grady. "You're obviously anorexic. I already found out you're getting weighed by the nurse. You got weighed just this morning, right?"

"You know, that's rude." Pearl's voice sprang out, hot. "That's none of your business."

"Really? Then maybe *you* should be the one getting weighed."

Gwendolyn smiled, victorious, as Pearl's face slammed shut, humiliated into silence. Oh, jeez. Grady's hands fluttered into the air like frightened birds, he had to grab them, hold one in the other.

Crunching his left hand with his right, he cracked his knuckles—and a sharp, satisfying *pop-snapple-pop* sang out. Gwendolyn, her leg swinging harder, rolled her eyes, disgusted. Pearl fought a lopsided grin off her lips. Then—failure—a giggle escaped and a squeak jumped out. Grady's own mouth twitched, a strange effervescence expanding quickly through his chest, rising up through his throat like fast yeast. A *laugh*.

Pearl's face turned red, her eyes giddy.

Grady laughed outright—a strange, harsh bark that made Gwendolyn look at him in horror, and made Pearl collapse in her chair, sliding down, her rear end traveling forward, her legs stretching ahead and toppling the portfolio—her body shaking, breasts jiggling. Before he could stop it, another bark jumped from his mouth, then another. Oh jeez, oh shit, when had he ever laughed so hard before? Oh Christ, oh golly, oh molly, oh holly—

The door to Mr. Edrickson's office opened, and the vice-principal's pudgy face popped out. Glaring, he stopped them cold. Gwendolyn smiled, triumphant.

Then Fred was filing out of Mr. Edrickson's office with an elderly woman. So who was she—his grandmother? Where were his parents?

Grady sat as still as possible, watching Fred's carefully blank face.

See, I can look at Fred, he reasoned to himself. It doesn't mean anything, he's just a guy, he's just—

He saw Fred's eyes flicker over the three of them as he passed, saying nothing. Saw him glance back. Then Fred and the woman moved through the door leading out of the front office, and disappeared.

Grady turned and saw three people standing and talking quietly to Mr. Edrickson. A short, slender African-American man, neatly dressed in a business suit—no dreads in sight—nodded gravely at the vice-principal. Jess in a hundred years, maybe, if he got religion. Beside him stood a slight, dark woman in a blue dress, her hair short and sleek and wavy. That had to be Jess's mother, she had the same eyes and mouth. The third person, a lanky white guy, stood slightly to the side. Wearing a pink shirt and dark green tie, his stomach bulging over his belt, an earring glinting in his ear, he wore his graying hair pulled back into a ponytail.

The three shook hands solemnly with Mr. Edrickson and started their exit, the white guy placing his hand on the shoulder of the black woman as they moved across the room, then moving his hand across her back to her other shoulder, ending up with his arm around her, their bodies pressed comfortably together as they walked. *Moby Dick.*

And then Mr. Edrickson was signaling him and Pearl and Gwendolyn to come inside. Grady's stomach twisted and he didn't move. No matter how much Jess might deserve it, how could he witness his moment of humiliation?

Then he found himself upright, Pearl pushing him along. Her hand on his elbow felt like fire or ice, he couldn't tell which, he only knew it hurt. But he didn't remove her hand, didn't jerk away. He moved through a hazy remembrance of the Group, talking and laughing, touching, the casual touching that happens between friends, on the arm or elbow, on the shoulder. He had touched all of them at one time or other, he was sure of it. He had wanted to touch Tracy even more, hadn't he?

Who would he touch now, though, if he *could* touch someone, and wanted to? Someone like Pearl, with her soft breasts and thighs? Or someone like Fred, with his boy's face and muscles, his fists? And who—

Target—

— would want to touch him?

Then he was in the room. Jess's frightened eyes—dark brown, almost black—grabbed him clear across the room and yanked him close, demanding his allegiance.

Grady gave it at once.

TWENTY

They sat in a small, uncomfortable circle, waiting. Mr. Edrickson cleared his throat. "As you know, you're here because we don't tolerate verbal insult and abuse here at Jefferson. When someone steps too far over the line, they have to pay the price for incivility. Right?" He looked at Jess.

Jess sat slumped in his chair, arms crossed, a tight, fake smile on his face, his eyes flooded with humiliation.

"Now," Mr. Edrickson continued, "we all make mistakes. The thing we have to do is remember to be fair and reasonable, to treat others the way we want to be treated ourselves. Right?" He looked at Jess, and Jess refreshed his smile, dropping it as soon as Mr. Edrickson looked away. "Now, I believe Jess has some words of apology." He turned to Jess expectantly.

Jess hesitated, struggling for control.

"Okay," he started—then stopped as a little rustling of paper filled the air. Pearl, her rosebud mouth shut tight in concentration, earnestly tore fine, tiny strips of paper back from a pack of Lifesavers, trying to pry out a candy. Suddenly aware of her audience, she stopped. "Oh," she said, popping an illicit orange in her mouth. "Sorry." She held out the pack, waving it slightly. "Anybody want one?"

"Yeah. Don't mind if I do." Jess.

Pearl handed the pack to Gwendolyn, who, legs crossed, top leg swinging, took it with disdain and handed it on to Jess. He rooted for the next candy. "Oh, good—cherry. My favorite." He tossed it in his mouth. "Know what I hate? Green. I mean, what flavor *is* green, anyway?" He passed the pack to Mr. Edrickson, who hesitated a moment, then handed it to Grady.

Grady froze, the cylinder of candy clutched in his hand. Should he take one?

"Well?" Mr. Edrickson looked at Jess.

Jess nodded, misery reasserting itself. "Okay, I said things last week I shouldn't have, things like—" he glanced at Mr. Edrickson—"well, I mean, I insulted everybody. And—I was wrong, okay? Everybody's got feelings and shi—I mean stuff. So, all right, I wasn't thinking. I was stupid. And, so, all right—I'm sorry." He leaned back in his chair, task completed.

Mr. Edrickson looked around the room. "Well?"

Gwendolyn snorted, her crossed leg swinging harder. "Some apology. I mean, you talk about our sex parts like that's all we are, and you call Fred a bad word right to his face. You really showed *your* true colors, Jess. I should think an African American like you—it's like you haven't learned anything, it's like you think sexism and homophobia are okay. And you can't fool me, you might have said the words but you aren't acting the least bit sorry. You haven't changed a bit. If *this* is what you call an apology—"

"Yeah," Jess said, leaning forward, his eyes narrowing. "It *is* what I call an apology. And my color, by the way, is black. Now, just for the record, what do you call snooping around in everybody's private business?"

"I've never *snooped*!" Gwendolyn retorted. "The *Journal*, for those of you who haven't been listening, is running a contest about new students. I just happen to be good at finding things out—*true* things."

"Hey!" Mr. Edrickson held his hand up in the air. "It's obvious you two have some other issues. If necessary, we'll deal with them right in this office. But today our focus is on Jess's apology for last week. Pearl? Grady?"

Huh? Grady found himself wrestling with the cylinder of Life-savers, Pearl holding the unopened end, his own fingers tangled in silver and waxy paper. The next candy was green. He lobbed it into his mouth.

What was he supposed to say? *Green* nuked his tonsils. Jess was right. Just what flavor was green?

"Fine," said Pearl, hiding the guilty pack of candy, with its trailing paper ribbons, in her hand. "I mean, it's okay. He apologized. And like you said, we all make mistakes. So, okay, maybe Jess sometimes isn't so, um, nice." She glanced at Jess uncertainly, then looked Mr. Edrickson. "But he writes poetry."

Grady gagged on his Lifesaver. Jess, his dark eyes springing wide, opened his mouth silently, his real face shocked into view—rage and humiliation scrambling for cover.

Gwendolyn, stilling her leg for a moment, snickered. "Oh," she said. "Poetry. Like, wow." Her leg started up again in swing time. "That explains everything. Lord Byron himself, right here at Jefferson."

Pearl looked desperately at Grady. "No, what I mean is—" She looked at Jess, dismay blanching her skin. "What I meant was—"

Mr. Edrickson cleared his throat. "It doesn't matter, Pearl. We all have our hobbies. Poetry is certainly a good one. Now, we came here today for an apology, and Jess gave it. We'll see what happens over the next several days. I'm hoping not to see any of you back here for this same reason. Okay?"

"And Gwendolyn." Mr. Edrickson paused until she looked at him. "This is a private matter. You're not to discuss it, or put what was said here, in any article you might write for the *Journal*. Understand?"

Then Grady was moving, herded out the door with Jess and Pearl, Pearl's face now blotched red with disaster. "What I meant was—" She reached to touch Jess's sleeve, but he jerked away, cutting her off, his eyes furious.

"What you meant was, you stuck your stupid face in my business. Now I suggest you go stick it in somebody else's." He glared at Grady, as if he, too, were a coconspirator in deceit. Then he left, his exit as fast as Gwendolyn's. Grady's fingers flew to his buttons. He watched as Pearl's eyes flooded with tears. Oh, jeez.

Exploring his jeans, his fingers found the wadded-up handkerchief Jess had given him last Friday in the library, still jammed in his pocket. He handed it to Pearl, who took it and held it against her face.

At least he could do that.

They parted, Pearl's face surfacing from the handkerchief long enough to whisper a tear-strangled *bye*. Trudging down the hall, Grady looked for a water fountain. *Green* was making him sick.

The entire class went quiet that afternoon when Jess walked into the room, everyone swinging around to look at Fred. But Fred studied the table in front of him as if it would answer all his questions as soon as he thought of some to ask. He didn't look up.

Jess sauntered to their table, smacked Grady on the arm, meaning, *Move over, dork. You're in my seat.* Grady slid over.

Jess got Grady his piece of paper and charcoal, then slapped one of his Wild Things paintings on the table. He began to paint a slight, brown-skinned woman in a blue dress, with sleek, wavy, short black hair.

When Pearl turned to her picture of the man, Grady cleared his throat. "Um, who? Is it?" His hands trembled.

Pearl waited, apparently debating whether to tell or not. In a hesitant voice, she said, "My father." Something dark swam up through her eyes. "He left," she said, the dark thing almost surfacing. "Three years ago." Then she shrugged, and the dark thing vanished.

"Um."

"I haven't seen him since. Except twice." She studied the still life in front of Grady, which today featured dark, oblong purple grapes, as yet unravished by Jess. "Can I have one?" Surprised, he nodded, and she reached and plucked one off. Hesitating, she handed it to him, her eyebrows raised in question. But he didn't know how to respond, so she set it on his piece of paper and plucked off another one for herself, then started to work on her drawing.

Grady stared at the purple grape, wondering about putting it in his mouth, biting into its sweetness. Did it have seeds? Probably. They'd have to be picked out, they'd have to be—

A brown hand streaked in front of him, grabbed the grape and disappeared it.

Grady picked up his piece of charcoal, and drew a grape.

He didn't look at Fred. Except once. Caught *him* looking at Jess, his face painted with uncertainty. How had their Apology Session gone?

He reached for his charcoal again, then felt a little nudge on his arm. A small, folded-up piece of paper bearing the name *Jess* slid in front of him. Pearl, her mouth tight, was silent. He slid the folded paper over to Jess, nudged *his* arm.

Jess eyed the square of paper, eyed Grady, frowned at Pearl, then opened it and read. His face blank, he crumpled it up and turned back to his painting. Grady could feel Pearl deflate; he hoped she didn't cry. Her face red, she turned back to her drawing.

Ten minutes later, engrossed in the task of filling his entire sheet of paper up with black, oblong grape-circles, Grady felt a nudge on his arm, saw a little square of paper bearing the name *Pearl* slide in front of him. He continued it on its journey, tapping Pearl's arm with his piece of charcoal, too timid to touch her with his fingers. He watched her open it, read something, then glance at Jess, who was busy again with his picture, sketching in what might be called A Portrait of the Grim Reaper as a Young Brother— Max, presumably, his lifted scythe aimed at the slight brown woman's neck. The Wild Thing gone bad.

It beat drawing a bunch of stupid grapes.

Grady tried to read the note over Pearl's shoulder, but it was at the wrong angle. Then she tucked it into her jeans pocket, picked up her pencil, and returned to her drawing.

And? So? Truce? Why didn't anybody ever tell him anything?

Class ended: Jess put his stuff away, turned in Grady's pathetic grape drawing, and exited, followed by Pearl.

Grady sat rooted, not knowing why. Most of the class left, Gwendolyn smirking at him on her way out. No, wait, she turned back, walking to the other side of the room to talk to Ms. Spencer, who was engrossed in conversation with some lingering kids. They stood pretty far away; it was a big room. He continued to sit, not knowing why. And then he knew why.

Fred had stayed behind, finishing up what he was doing, now scraping the wood shavings off the table into his cupped hand and walking to the big trash can on Grady's side of the room. Navy blue shirt. Brown, crazy-combed hair. Wire rims.

Grady found himself standing, found himself moving toward Fred. He stopped, almost close to him, and waited.

Fred, still occupied with the trash can, brushed shavings off his palm. Then he turned, looked up and jerked back, alarm surging over his face. Quickly regaining composure, he shifted to a more subdued suspicion. "Well?" he asked.

Grady's face grew hot, sweat dampening his armpits. Fred's expression was one of hostile scrutiny, of readiness for what was necessary—fight or flight. He wasn't showing Grady a face of understanding, a face of *knowledge*, but a face of armed defense, his light-brown eyes hardened and waiting.

Grady stumbled for a button, then another one, rushing desperately from button surface to button surface, uncomfored. He finally stuck his hands in his jeans pockets. "Um . . ."

He tried to regroup, but only succeeded in shutting his eyes. Well, this was stupid. He opened them again. The light in the room—a mild, quiet, almost-November afternoon light—filled him. How had November crept so close, so silently?

November.

The month when everything happened, almost a year ago.

After which everything was *After*.

Well, maybe Fred did know something. Grady glanced quickly across the room to make sure Gwendolyn was still safely far away, but only the other kids were present, excitedly and loudly hashing something out. He heard Ms. Spencer's voice rise above theirs. Gwendolyn must have given up and left.

He turned to Fred, voice thick. "I have to do this paper." Many words needed to follow, an impossible number of words. "For Sociology." Lie. He wasn't taking Sociology. "About, um." He stopped. "About, um."

Fred coughed. "Look," he began, pushing his fingers through his hair. "I've got some friends waiting—"

"About, you know. Rape."

Fred pulled back.

"I mean. What I mean is." Grady's voice sounded like old, rusty nails rattling together in a coffee can. "When men do it. I mean—to other men." Grady pushed the word-nails out of his mouth, hammering. He didn't know where they came from, or what they were building. "I read this article in the paper. A year ago. About some guy who was, you know." A whole flock of words, Grady could see them now—not nails anymore but birds, rising into the air, moving across the sky. Hungry birds, dark ones—each one frantic, starved for food. "Raped. Around here."

Fred stepped farther away.

Grady forced himself to continue. "I thought. You might—um. Know something. Because you're, I mean, because you're, you know, gay, and you might," he swallowed, his saliva as thick as cement, "know something." He touched his lip with his tongue, it had split open again, and he saw that Fred's face had turned hard, his anger a brick about to be thrown.

Oh, jeez.

Grady tried to inhale. Dizziness blurred his vision, he had to sit down. He slid onto a stool, listening to Fred's silence. Lowering his head to his hand, he stared at the tabletop.

When it came, Fred's voice was cold. "I get it. Ask the resident *homo* about something like that, as if I walk around knowing all about that kind of crap. Like I'm gay, so I got born knowing shit like that? Like I'm—like gay people are rape *specialists* or something, like that's what we do in our spare time—go around raping each other? *Jesus Christ*! What the—" He stopped, his voice a razor—it cut flesh. Grady felt it slide under his skin, peel him like a grape. Dark birds cried, circling over his head.

"What the hell kind of people do you think we are?"

Grady couldn't answer, could barely breathe.

"Go ask some of your homophobic friends, okay? *They'd* know more about it than I do. *They're* the kind of people who do that kind of shit. Just leave me alone! You got that?"

"No," Grady said. "That's not—no. I didn't mean . . . ." Well, what had he meant? He became silent, issuing no words. He had none.

And suddenly the blond-haired man was kneeling over him, laughing. Grady felt his hand squeezing his neck, his breath hot and stinking in his face, his knee pressed against his stomach, squeezing his insides up into his lungs until he couldn't breathe. "Shit," the dark-haired man laughed. "You're a fucking piece of shit."

His eyes closed, his face wet with tears, Grady suddenly understood that whatever the two men were, they were crazy. High Fucking Crazy. Shit-to-Shit Fucking Crazy. Grady their shit masterpiece, their self-portrait. Their three-person self-portrait of shit, Grady's contribution his body. Shit, all of them. Shit.

He lifted his head. The room, now silent, was empty, dappled with a quiet, almost-November afternoon light. Fred had gone. The men had gone. He used his sleeve to wipe his face. He had to begin his walk to the library.

No, he was wrong, the room wasn't empty. Ms. Spencer's faraway voice came into focus. Grady stood slowly, turning slightly—and saw Fred. He'd merely stepped aside, out of his line of vision.

Fred studied him uncertainly, the anger on his face all

117

botched-up with confusion. He looked at the floor, then back. "Look," he started—but a cough turned his head, and Grady's eyes followed.

Gwendolyn sat at a table behind them, eyeing Grady with a somber triumph. "Interesting little research paper you're doing there," she said. "Guys raping guys." She shuddered. "Kind of gross, though. Heck, I'd cry, too. That must have been some newspaper article you read. Although *I* wouldn't assume a gay person would like, *do* that sort of thing, just because he's gay. I mean, surely we've moved beyond that." She smiled at Fred, then turned back to Grady. "And you're doing this paper for Sociology, which is interesting, since I happen to know you're not taking Sociology." She grinned, pleased with her own intelligence report. "I'd call that *real* interesting."

Pain exploded in Grady's gut, vomit surging to his mouth and dribbling down his chin as he ran for the door. "Hey!" Gwendolyn yelled, her voice disappearing behind his back.

He galloped, a crazy, clumsy horse, down the hall until he spotted a utility closet door. Clawing at it—miraculously, it opened—he jumped through, banging into mops and brooms and pails. He slammed the door behind him, shutting himself up inside a small, smelly darkness. Crouched on the crowded floor, panting, he held himself still until the only thing between him and blackness was nothing.

He lay sprawled on the floor until a maintenance man opened the door. "What the hell—" he said. Grady stood up, blinking stupidly, and wobbled his way down the hall.

Head aching, Grady went to bed as soon as he got home. He woke in the middle of the night, his sheet glued to his body with sweat. A fire burned just under his skin. He knew it would never go out, would burn him up until he was dead. Relieved, he closed his eyes and let the fire blaze.

In the morning, his fever spiking, his mother made him stay home from school. She stayed home, too, bringing him Tylenol and icy Cokes, then cold, sweet green grapes.

Grady slipped a CD into his player and listened to the Country Gentlemen sing "Bringing Mary Home." Mary, the little girl killed on the highway, who every year, on the anniversary of her death, reappeared beside the road, begging to be taken home.

Every year, someone stopped to give her a ride.

And every year, as they turned into her driveway, she disappeared.

Grady was disappearing, too.

Grady spent the next day sleeping. By late afternoon, he felt better. He even, for the first time since forever, turned on his bedroom light. He wasn't sure why. All it did was illuminate things—bed, desk, chair. Clothes and junk strewn about. Nightstand. Phone, the ringer turned off. Unread books. TV tray. Computer.

Computer. Dust covered it, like it covered everything—a dry, silky kind of touching. Not the kind of touching he used to imagine when he surfed the net for porn, at least for what he could get without a credit card. One of his favorite, even if nervewracking, occupations, *Before*. Now an impossibility, the reason he couldn't touch his computer.

With his fever subsiding, he watched his mother relax her grieving, My-Son-Is-Dying vigilance and assume a plucky-hen strut: She'd done the mother thing, it had worked.

That evening he sat in bed, propped against pillows, his long legs stretched under the blankets, working on the bowl of cream of mushroom soup delivered half an hour ago, trying not to spill it all over his comforter. He still felt weak; his mother told him he had to stay home tomorrow.

His father, napkin crumpled in his fist, stuck his head around the doorway of his bedroom. "Grady, you've got a call. She didn't identify herself."

Grady almost dropped the bowl in his lap. A call? No one phoned him anymore, ever. And from a *she*?

His father waited for a response, obviously pleased to be

standing in a lighted room instead of a semidark one. Grady set the bowl down on the TV tray and reached to pick up the receiver, waiting pointedly for his father to leave the room.

"Hello?" His voice came out like a fog blanketing the sea.

"Grady?" Small voice cutting through the fog. Grady pretended he didn't recognize Pearl's voice.

"Who?"

"It's me. I mean, Pearl." Silence. "You okay?"

"Yes. Had a fever." How'd she get his number?

"I see. You coming back tomorrow?"

"No. Thursday." He was pretty sure.

"Oh. Well."

Silence. So why had she called, if she didn't have anything to say? "So, um, how was school?" Doing his part, his voice breaking into little jagged pieces.

"Okay." Silence. "I found out who that woman was. You know, that old woman with Fred yesterday? Some kind of third cousin twice removed or something. He lives with her now, because his parents kicked him out, because he's gay and everything. Well, that's what I heard." Gossip update, followed by silence.

Grady really didn't want to hear about Fred right now. And he'd already figured out the woman wasn't his mother, so it was hardly news.

"Well, I called because I came up with a self-portrait of three people idea." Anxious voice followed by pause. Grady imagined her lips tightening into a protective pink bud. "Jess thinks it's stupid."

So they were talking—it *was* a truce. "Oh. What, um, is it?"

"Well." Grady heard a small swell of pride in her voice. "See, what I thought was, instead of doing one portrait of three people, why not do three portraits of one person?"

"Um."

"Okay, what I mean is, we choose one of us—except I think it should be you, because you're in the middle, kind of, and we both like you. Well, what I mean is, it's not that I *like* you, I just think you're, um, nice. I mean —"

Grady listened to her voice scramble for cover. He waited, tense.

"What I mean is, me and Jess don't get along real well, so it has to be you. He called me 'fatso' today, so I don't really want to see his portrait of me." Silence. "Well, okay, then he said he was sorry, except I don't think he really was. He had that *Jess* look, you know? But I don't care, not really. I mean, I know I'm fat, so it's not like he was wrong."

Grady could hear the hurt in her voice. But what could he say? She wasn't exactly thin. But then—she wasn't exactly *fat*, either. Not really. Maybe a little.

He remembered the drunk party girl. Her lips had been narrow, not like Pearl's rosebud. And her body—

"Grady? You still there? So, what we do is three portraits of you. Okay?"

"Uh." Grady tried to remember how to breathe.

"See, if we each do a portrait of you, we'll each do it differently, right? We're three different people, so the way the pictures turn out will be, like, a portrait of *us*. Get it?"

Got it. "I don't know." Grady's fingers researched the quilt on his bed—full and soft, stuffy with, um, stuff. Grady, his face hot, wondered if his temperature had come back.

"Well, I just mean—" Grady heard tears somewhere in her voice. Then, "Okay, Jess was right. It's stupid."

"No. It's just, um."

"No, it's stupid. Sorry. Sorry I called and bothered you."

Click.

Dial tone.

Grady held the receiver in his hand, then set it down. Leaning back against his pillow, he discovered he'd dribbled mushroom soup down the front of his T-shirt. He rubbed as much of it off as he could with a napkin, then closed his eyes, bumping against the edges of sleep.

Fred's real-life face appeared. Different from his dream-face, it told him nothing about who or what he, Grady, was. So—was he a guy who used to like girls, but a guy who, one night on a dark road, had lost the right to ever look at a girl again?

If so, who was he supposed to look at now?

He opened his eyes, his room a quiet, illuminated monument to solid objects. But what about things that aren't solid, that shift around, that change shape and meaning? What about them? He let his eyes shut, and found himself back with Fred.

He couldn't imagine kissing him. Or—he traced the surface of Fred's face, his dream-face, with his fingertips—maybe he could.

Grady didn't understand any of this. Just before falling asleep, he realized he was falling asleep.

"Grady, you have another call. Same person, I think." His father stood in the doorway, curiosity open on his face. "Who is it, anyway? I made the mistake again of not asking, and your mother just about killed me. She's all but rolling on the floor right now with frustration."

Grady peered at the clock. About an hour had passed since Pearl had hung up. "Oh." He cleared his throat. "It's nobody. Just some girl from school."

"Well, I figured that. So her name's *nobody*, huh?" He chuckled. "Your mother's going to be thrilled with that piece of information. I'll never be allowed to answer the phone again." He rubbed his eyes and half-laughed, and Grady noted the lines on his face.

Turning to leave, he paused. "You want another Coke?" Grady shook his head no, and when his father left, picked up the receiver.

"Sorry I hung up on you my idea was stupid but I shouldn't have hung up like that it was rude I'm sorry." Pearl on speed.

"Um, no. It's okay."

"No, it isn't okay." She sounded miserable.

"No, it is, really." Silence. "It's just that—I don't want three portraits of me."

"Oh. Why?"

Grady thought of Fred, kicked out by his parents, and Gwendolyn, her mean eyes. Tracy. The Group. Jess, his dark brown, almost black eyes, angry at every single white person in the entire world, but nonetheless probing him, demanding entrance. Pearl, her deep blue eyes full of shadows.

And the two men—their stinking breath, their tongues in his mouth.

What would any of them paint into his portrait, if they could actually see him? Paint so everyone would know?

A portrait of shit. A shit masterpiece.

"Grady?"

"Uh"—Grady heard birds somewhere, they were hungry and crying—"It's just—" Grady tried to speak, answer Pearl. "Because—then everyone would see."

"See what?"

"They'd see—what happened."

Silence.

"So—well, okay then." Pearl's voice was hesitant, distant and strange. "I mean—what happened?"

Grady's voice was just a whisper. "The *Night Of*."

"The—what?"

"The—" Grady's finger shook. His heart thick, his voice a bird flapping away into the sky, he forced the last words. "The *Night Of*. The night—I was raped."

Silence.

"Grady, did you say—"

Grady set down the phone.

THREE

Wednesday morning Grady's mother handed him a bowl of cream of celery soup for breakfast, setting a box of saltines on his tray. *Huh?* "We're out of cereal," she said. "But who says you can't have soup for breakfast?" She smiled. "I added real cream." Did she think that *real cream* would pack on the pounds? "It's good for you," she added emphatically.

O-o-kay.

He diddled around, adding enough crackers to make a castle-shaped mound in the middle of his bowl. Satisfied, he set it on his TV tray and fell asleep.

His mother shook him awake and handed him a bowl of cream of tomato. "Your mid-morning snack," she said, folding her arms and glaring.

"I'm feeling better now," he protested. Maybe she'd take the hint and leave, put in half a day at work, release him from this soup torture.

"*Eat.* Then go clean up and shave."

He got down a couple spoonfuls, then headed for the shower.

"Oh," she said, when he emerged from the bathroom, her arms full of his dirty sheets, "that friend of yours, Pearl, called back a third time last night, but you'd fallen asleep." His mother searched for his real face, but he kept it hidden. "She told me she's the third person in your art project." Silence. "Well, she gave me her phone number to give to you." She shifted the sheets in her arms and handed him a scrap of paper, then left.

Grady stuck the scrap under his newly dusted phone—his

mother must be having an extended Mother Moment—and crawled back into bed between clean sheets. Maybe his conversation with Pearl hadn't happened, maybe he'd dreamed it.

Her phone number a dream, too.

Grady reached for the smooth coolness of clean sheets—fresh, waiting to be touched. Had he really told Pearl what he told her? He couldn't have.

He deliberately closed his eyes. Falling asleep, he had a crazy dream about soup, about swimming in a deep, dark ocean of soup.

He never wanted to see a bowl of cream of *anything* again. Grady lay on top of his blankets in his sweats, ignoring his cream of potato and listening through his headphones to Grandpa Jones sing and joke about a hillbilly's first encounter with an indoor toilet. It was pretty funny.

Whap! What the—? Grady blinked, confused, and saw Jess standing beside his bed.

Jess.

Pulling his headphones off, Grady fought an awkward smile off his face.

"Yo, Bean Head." Jess studied the room critically. "Your basic suburban wasteland. At least you got the light turned on." He eyed the bowl of potato soup on the TV tray. "Munchkin soup? I'm a vegetable beef man, myself." He rummaged in the box of saltines, stuck one in his mouth.

"Your girlfriend—excuse me, I forgot you got a little confusion on that matter—*Pearl* told me you were sick. Said she talked to you last night."

Jess had talked to Pearl? Grady's chest tightened. Had Pearl told him? Surely she hadn't told him—

Panic strangled the air out of his lungs.

Jess reached into the cracker box again, helping himself to a handful of saltines, then pulled the desk chair over to the bed and sat down. He popped a couple of crackers in his mouth and chewed. "So, you coming back tomorrow?"

Grady, dragging air forcibly into his lungs, nodded.

"Good. Because—well, never mind."

Never mind? "What?" Grady's voice leapt from his mouth, a shriek.

Jess lifted his eyebrows. "Hey, don't go nuclear on me. I was just asking."

Clenched with anxiety, Grady tried to relax. But his muscles stayed tight. He needed surfaces, he needed—

"But this might interest you." Jess stuck another cracker in his mouth, licking salt off his fingers. "Guess who comes up to me at the beginning of art today? Fred the Fag. Oh, excuse me—*Fred.*" Jess's face chafed at his verbal leash, his lips scrunched up in disgust. But then something uncomfortable seemed to walk across his face, and his eyes traveled to the ceiling, studying it intensely. Then he looked at Grady and shrugged. "Well, he's okay, I guess. I mean, if you got to be that way."

Grady about fell off the bed.

"For real, if I gotta get beat up by a homo, I'd choose Fred every time." Jess gnawed on another cracker. "I mean, when he bent over so I could kiss his ass in front of his granny, or whoever she was, make my own private Rainbow Coalition of a family proud to see how well their son can kiss butt, Fred didn't even fart in my face. So that's something."

Grady tried to recover, gain control over his breath. This breath, in, for—

"So anyway, he comes up to me and the whole class is watching us, like I'm really gonna volunteer to get my head busted a second time. I mean, shit, I'm not that dumb.

"So there I was being polite, acting all sensitive." Jess cracked his knuckles. "Being nice to the gayly disposed. But Fred cuts me off like a piece of moldy salami, says he just wants to know where you are. Says he's got something for you."

Grady kept his face still.

"So, um." Jess chewed a fingernail, eyeing Grady carefully. "You don't got something, you know, *going* with him, do you?"

Air exploded from Grady's lungs. Choking, he leaned forward, his chest strangled.

"That a yes or a no?" Jess stood up and grabbed Grady by the shoulder, slamming him on the back with his fist: First Aid Karate for lungs. Pounded him again. Remained in position until Grady stopped coughing and wheezed his way back to normal breath.

Jess sat back down. "Man, you don't do *nothing* half way." He watched as Grady leaned back against his pillows. "And the winner is? Mind you, I'm just asking." Jess rubbed his nose. "I mean, if you've really gone homo on me, I got to keep up all this sensitivity shit, right? But hey, I can do it, I'm a rehabilitated, modern man. Bring on the fat chicks and queers." He waited. "Well?"

Grady closed his eyes. Well?

He opened them, the light in the room harsh. "Um. No." The light didn't change.

"Oh. Well, good. Thought maybe you'd turned into the world's skinniest fag. Excuse me, homosexual. Not to mention the tallest. You know, you should seriously consider weight gain as an extracurricular activity. Maybe you and Pearl can arrange a fat transfer. Get written up in *People*, write a book, go on talk shows and make a kazillion dollars." Jess sniffed, staring at the floor. "So what's Fred got for you?" He raised his eyes to Grady.

"Don't know."

Jess lifted his eyebrows.

Grady's fingers stroked the surface of his blankets. Smoothly rough, or roughly smooth.

"Well, before you go psycho on me with the fingers—"

"I, um. Talked to him." He looked at Jess. No, Pearl hadn't told him, he could tell. Jess didn't know anything. "Talked. That's all." He shifted his eyes away.

Silence.

A blast of air burst from Jess's mouth. "You *talked* to him. Did the ole move-the-mouth thing. The Grady-man has finally *spoken*. To Fred. Well, okay, it's a Special Agent's job to encourage communication. With whomever. Yes, indeed, it is." He scrunched up his nose, shifting his eyes away, and for a moment Grady saw something like hurt flicker across his face. "Of course, all *I* ever get from you is a variation on the word 'um,' but maybe that's enough for the brother. Am I right?"

Grady watched Jess's eyes turn black, saw the fire raging behind them.

No.

But silence filled him up like bad air.

"Okay, then." Jess stood up, flushed with anger. "I'm outta here."

"Wait." Words, hundreds of them—but he had no voice. Birds flapped across the sky, hungry and searching.

Jess stood still, his face careful.

"Something happened." Birds shrieked in Grady's ears, he wanted them to stop.

Jess waited.

"A year ago." Grady didn't take his eyes off Jess, he couldn't.

Jess shifted his weight. "Yeah, well, I kind of figured that. You're pretty much a walking advertisement for disaster. So—what happened?"

Grady kept his eyes on Jess—but Jess now stood too far away, he could barely see him. A bird forced its way out of Grady's mouth—how did it get there?

"Rape," it cawed, softly.

Jess rubbed his eyes, frowning. "What?"

Another bird burst out, wheeling across the sky. "Rape," it cried, but Grady could barely hear it. Water fell down his face, a storm had darkened the sky, it was raining.

Jess chewed his lower lip, his eyes puzzled. "Rape? You know someone who was raped?" An unidentified emotion danced across his skin. "Well, that's pretty bad, all right. So—who was she?" He stood a long minute inside Grady's silence, then finally sighed. "Well, don't go telling me everything at once now." He reached into his pocket, pulled out a handkerchief and handed it over. Grady clutched it in his fist. "You got this crying stuff bad, buddy. You could start a business selling other people's handkerchiefs. Not that I'm complaining."

The sky turned black, filling up with screaming, diving birds. Grady rolled away from Jess, pulled a pillow over his head.

A moment later he felt Jess flick his finger, hard, against his arm, branding—all the way down through his sweats—his skin.

"Okay, Bean Head," he heard him say. "It's okay. We can do the talk thing later." Silence. "See you tomorrow, then—okay?"

Okay.

Grady slept, his dreams filled up with nothing.

Freshly weighed by Mrs. Nurse—who'd frowned and asked him again when his appointment with Dr. Wonderful was—Grady sat in homeroom and pretended not to feel lightheaded and sick to his stomach.

Jess walked in late, hesitated, then took the empty seat next to Grady, eyeing him briefly. He opened his composition book and started writing, then leaned back, reading it over.

Grady snuck a look. Amid scratched-out words and hatch marks, sat a poem.

> girl, i will funk you black
> stars of darkness glitter
> in your soul
> the deep black night
> not half so deep as you
>
> girl, funk me back
> travel with me into night's
> dark face
> the luminescent moon
> not half so beautiful as you

Grady stared at the words. *Wow.*

Jess glanced up. "Fuck!" he yelled, slamming his book shut, his eyes two blowtorches. Everyone in the room turned around.

"Problem there?" The teacher stared over his bifocals.

"No. No problem." Fury spilled from Jess's face. "Sorry." The necessary contrition bit. Grady, cringing, remained silent.

"Okay, then." The teacher gave them both a hard look, then turned to the whole class. "I'm supposed to give these out. They didn't give me enough, so you'll have to share."

A minute later, Grady found himself holding a flyer from the *Jefferson Journal*. "The New Student Contest is almost over! But we still need a few more new students to come forward and tell their stories—one of you will actually win something! (Soon as we decide what!) But you've got to do it quick, time's running out, and soon you won't be new anymore!"

"Oh, like, duh."

Grady discovered Jess reading over his arm.

"And man, what kind of shit is that?" Jess flicked the bottom of the page, mocking the printed words in a singsong voice. "'Guys raping guys—it happens, and right in this area! Is this a serious threat for teens, or just another exaggerated danger? Check out the *Journal* next Tuesday for an up-to-date examination of this hot topic!'" Jess stuck his finger in his mouth, pretending to gag. "What a fucking load of crap. That's got to be Gwendolyn's work, I know how she thinks."

Grady's throat tightened and his hands shook, he had to put the flier down.

Please, no.

He needed to leave at once, run away, push on to someplace else. The bell rang, and Grady found himself upright and moving.

Jess smacked his arm. "See you at lunch."

At lunch? Grady moved through the halls, the shadow of a bird darkening the wall beside him.

As his unwrapped ice-cream sandwich softened toward meltdown, Grady listened to the silence that lay just beneath the loud shouts and clanging of dishes and trays that filled the cafeteria. Did anyone else hear it? It was the same silence that had wrapped itself around his heart the first time Mr. Howell had touched him.

He closed his eyes, not bothering to play his Blue Highway CD. He wasn't a different person, he'd never be.

He heard the scrape of chairs, looked up to see Jess park himself across the table. To Grady's surprise, the small black girl with the piled-up, blonde-tinged hair also sat down. Jess raised his eyebrows and smiled. "This is Darla. I believe I've mentioned her to you."

Grady sat up straighter. Had Jess written his poem for her? He nodded. "Um."

Darla nodded back, smiling politely. Up close, Grady could see that her eyes were dark and almond shaped, slanted upward at the ends, her mouth full and painted a dark plum color. Her skin darker than Jess's.

Tiny body, short tight clothes.

"She knows you got a tongue problem, so it's not like we're expecting major conversation here." Jess eyed the ice-cream sandwich. "You eating that? It's just about melted."

Grady shook his head no, and Jess grabbed it. "I'm just checking to see that you're not gonna cut out on me today." He turned to Darla, offering her a bite. She shook her head no and Jess proceeded to demolish it, the soft vanilla oozing out between chocolate cake layers.

Grady's fingers traveled over his jean-clad thighs. Frustrated, he grabbed his thighs and squeezed. Why didn't—

"You gonna show up in art?"

"Yes." What was the big deal?

"Good."

"Why?"

Jess licked ice cream off his fingers and shrugged. "Well, you know. We got to think about that three-person thing. I guess you heard Pearl's idea. I mean, it sucks, but so does the whole concept, you know? Besides, I can't think of anything else do to, seeing as *my* idea got me beaten up. Not to mention thrown in the Jefferson jail. Not to mention reprimanded for life." He sniffed. "Unless we want to make one of those voodoo doll things, make it look like Ms. Spencer and stick it full of pins. Man, I used to *respect* that woman." He crumbled up the ice-cream wrapper and tossed it at Darla, grinning. She pretended to dodge, then picked the wad up off the table and rolled her eyes.

"Okay, just stopping by. Me and Darla got to go grab some grub. See you in art, okay?"

Grady nodded, watched the two stand up and leave, saw Darla chuck the wadded wrapper back at Jess as they exited.

He stared at the table.

False advertising: Nobody talked about the three-way portrait. Not Jess, his head bent over his Wild Things painting. Not Pearl, wearing the blue denim jumper-thing again, a long-sleeved, light orange T-shirt covering her arms.

He'd activated his Pearl Management Program the minute he'd walked into the room: He ignored her. Except right at the beginning, when his hands shook badly and she slipped him a rope of licorice to hang on to, rubbing and stretching it until his fingers relaxed. He'd pretty much had to give her a thank-you smile. But he ignored the anxious smile on *her* face—confusion wrestling openly with worry—and turned away.

The still life in front of him was just rocks now—Jess had eaten the apple as soon as he walked in. He glanced across the room. Gwendolyn sat by herself, Fred missing. Deliberately breaking his stick of charcoal in half, Grady imagined slipping a razor-sharp knife under her skin, peeling back her whiteness, slicing the pale blue right out of her eyes, and giving it to the birds—a new sky they could fly in.

He blinked, made himself breathe.

Why wasn't Fred in class? What did he have for him? Well, he'd never know now, too bad. Relief softened the tension in his arms, then he found himself stifling disappointment.

He watched Jess go through his Wild Things paintings. He had created a whole new version of *Where the Wild Things Are*: Max Meets King Kong, Max Meets Godzilla, Max Meets Mom and Lops Off Her Head, Max Meets Dad, Max Meets the Lanky White Guy with the Ponytail and Throttles Him, Max Meets Ms. Spencer, Max Meets Gwendolyn and Her Bright Red Pubic Hair. Scenarios Sendak had overlooked. So far, Grady and Pearl remained MIA. Fred, too, which was surprising. Surely he'd be the worst Wild Thing of all.

Jess hadn't laid in the story yet, the actual words. Grady had a feeling he'd change those, too. He didn't remember anything in Sendak's text like *funk you black*.

Jess started to paint in a new Wild Thing, a chunky little white girl. Charlie, no doubt. Grady stared at his own blank piece of paper, at the two pieces of charcoal in his hand. And felt a nudge on his right arm.

A little square of folded-up paper sat beside his elbow, his name written across the top.

He glanced at Pearl, her eyes immediately jumping from his down to the drawing she was working on. He hesitated, then opened her note: *We need to talk, OK?* That was it. He felt Jess notice his movements and stop working, silently demand to know what Pearl had written. But Grady ignored him, pulled a pencil out of his pocket, then stopped. What could he say? No way he was actually going to "talk" with her. He'd just gone crazy or something the past two nights, with both her and Jess, maybe because he'd been sick.

OK, he wrote, in sprawling letters, folding the paper up and pushing it back. He'd just make up some story, tell her what he'd said was a joke. And besides, he'd be leaving the area soon anyway, maybe even tonight, he just needed to throw a few things together.

At the end of class, Jess and Pearl didn't leave. Perplexed,

Grady shifted on his stool. They always left before he did. What was going on?

"Come on, I'll give you a ride to the library," Jess said, giving orders.

"Um. No. That's all right."

"No, really, go with him." Tension had set up camp on Pearl's face. "I mean, I'm going, too."

Huh?

Jess cleared his throat. "Yeah. See, we talked while you were gone, and we've got to make some decisions about this three-person thing."

Weren't they supposed to have just done that? "No."

"Sorry." Jess clapped invisible handcuffs on Grady. "Special Agent Jess insists. Besides"—his eyes sparked with amusement—"I promised your mama I'd keep an eye on you."

What? Jess had talked to his *mother*?

"Hey, don't get mad at me. I was innocently making my way out your front door last night when she nabs me. I mean, I barely had my jacket on, when she drags me out on the porch and tells me about this big doctor's appointment you've got next week, except she's afraid you'll drop dead or something before you get there." Jess laughed. "See, I told you to join the after-school Fat Transfer Club. You'd get your picture in the yearbook and every-thing."

"You—" Grady's voice strangled in his throat.

"Come on, Grady, please." Pearl pleaded with her eyes.

Damn her. Damn Jess. Damn his stupid mother. He stared at the table, rage thick in his throat, listening to them not leave.

"Come on, Bean Head." Jess stood up, the pistol at Grady's back, and Pearl slid off her stool, her denim jumper-thing making a swoosh. *Okay.* He'd go along, listen to them talk about the stupid art thing till they got bored and left. Should take only about five minutes.

He followed Jess out the door, Pearl taking up the rear—and

immediately saw Fred, standing by himself a short ways down the hall, leaning against a locker, studying either his shoes or the floor. Jeans. Rust-colored sweater. Dark hair going every-which-way. Grady swallowed, his mouth suddenly dry. Fred hadn't been in class, what was he doing here now? He reached for a button—a cool, eternal, Zen button, a button representative of the universe.

Fred looked up at their approach, paused, then stepped in front of them, targeting Grady. "I've got something for you," he said, the hall thick with tension. Then he half-shrugged, allowing a small relaxation into the air. "I wasn't in class, I had a meeting." Words of explanation. He darted his eyes toward Jess, anxiety surfacing—but Jess didn't respond, his body still.

Hesitating a bare second, Fred handed Grady a small, white card. "I got this from somebody. It might help. You know, with your paper."

Grady looked down, found himself holding a business card, the words "Men's Health Center" printed in bold type. Below that, a name—Allan Reeve, LCSW—followed by a phone number and address.

Fred shrugged. "You can, you know, call. The person who gave it to me said this guy will talk to you, give you information and stuff. Maybe tell you where you can get, um"—he glanced at Jess—"help for your report." He licked his top lip. "You don't have to be—you know." His mouth tightened and he shrugged.

The card burned between Grady's fingers. "Thanks."

Fred nodded briefly, then turned to leave. When he looked back for just a moment, Grady lifted his hand—a stiff wave.

"So what was that all about? What did he give you?" Jess stared at the back of the card.

"Oh, uh, nothing." Grady stuck the card in his shirt pocket. "Nothing."

Jess snorted in disgust. "Right. And I'm Michael fucking Jordan, in drag." He shook his head. "Well, screw it. Go ahead and talk to everybody in the whole damn universe, everybody except me. What do I care?" He glared at Grady, his eyes bright with hurt, then turned sharply, stomping down the hall, dreads bouncing. He called back over his shoulder. "Is your stupid butt coming, or what?"

Grady and Pearl scrambled after him, Grady loping along as best as he could to keep up. The card blazed in his pocket.

Grady waited with Jess in front of the school in silent, shivering misery, the cool air whipped to a stiff chill by the breeze. Jess, his eyes still flashing *pissed* in brown neon, ignored him. He kept checking his watch and looking around, and finally Grady saw why. Darla sauntered up, her dark face vivid in the clear air. Jess changed immediately, dropping *pissed* for *hello!*

Darla nodded to Grady, said, "Hey." Grady nodded back.

"Got to make two stops before the library," Jess said, by way of explanation. "Drop Darla off at work, pick up Charlie. Won't take long."

Pearl hurried up, encased in a denim jacket, her portfolio in her arms. She stared at Darla—and suddenly got interested in her own feet, her dark, curly hair falling forward to hide her face.

"Darla, this is Pearl. Pearl, Darla." Jess dug for his keys. "Let's go, okay?" He turned as Darla and Pearl nodded to each other, and they all set off for the parking lot, finally stopping in front of an ancient Plymouth Reliant. Baby blue. Banged up and rusting where the paint had chipped. Totally untricked. Totally untrickable. Oh, man. How had Jess ended up with a mess like this? Grady felt a whole new sympathy.

They waited as Jess rearranged the junk in the back seat. When he finally pulled himself out, shaking back his dreads, he returned Grady's stare. "Well, what did you expect, an El Dorado? Maybe a bar in the back seat, chicks in the hot tub?" He snorted. "I mean, my *dad* picked it out. Got it cheap from some guy he works with." He laughed. "But, hey, he pays the insurance, so I'm not complaining."

There was enough room for two people to sit in the back, if they didn't mind being sardines. On Grady's right, lumped around an old computer so dead-looking all it needed was four little feet sticking up in the air, stretched an enormous pile of ratty clothes, books, old newspapers, empty soda cans, skin mag wannabes and junk food wrappers. To his left sat Pearl, smashed against his arm and thigh. He could hardly breathe.

As Darla slid into the front seat, which in contrast was pretty neat and tidy, Grady tried to calm down. Difficult to do with the hip-hop now detonating in his ears.

Wedged in next to Pearl, feeling the soft edge of her rear end and thigh smashed against his, Grady swallowed, trying to ignore the heat pressed between them, concentrating instead on the passing roads and traffic. They stopped in front of a small house, waited while Jess got out and came back, accompanied by Charlie—wearing her ugly puffy pink jacket, her nose running.

She climbed in the front seat and Darla slid to the middle, pressing close to Jess. Grady couldn't remember sitting that close to a girl—well, except for right now.

Jess turned the music down to a dull thump. "I'm on Charlie duty today," he said, flatly. "Don't even ask." He shook his head. "Charlie, say hi to Pearl. You've met Grady." He took off—if you can call taking off in a Reliant taking off.

Charlie waved shyly at Grady, grinned at Pearl, then turned to Darla. "Hi, Dar-la-la."

"Hey, baby. Do your nose, okay?" She handed Charlie a tissue.

They stopped at a strip mall, Darla and Charlie climbed out, Charlie climbed back in. "Thanks," said Darla, leaning back in before shutting the door, talking across Charlie to Jess. "See you later." Grady watched her dark eyes send him some kind of private telegram. Jess nodded, sending her an unspoken message back. Then Darla turned to Charlie. "Do your belt, baby."

"Okey-dokey, Dar-la-la." Charlie wiggled around with the seat belt.

Darla nodded at Grady and Pearl. "Nice meeting you. Good luck."

Good luck? With what? He locked his eyes on Charlie, twisted around as far as she could get in her seat belt.

"Dammit, Charlie. Quit staring. Didn't they teach you anything in socialization class this week?" Jess, his voice sharp, banged his thumbs against the steering wheel as he waited for a light.

"Got an *S* in reading today," Charlie said.

"There you go. I knew that sooner or later they'd figure out you're a genius."

Charlie twisted around again, smiling proudly at Grady and Pearl. "*S* means Satisfactory."

Grady felt a smile touch his lips. "Um," he said. "Good."

"Great!" shouted Pearl, making Grady jump. Then she turned red, picking at a button on her jacket. Did she really know about buttons?

"Yeah," said Jess, checking traffic before merging. "That's us—my whole family, a bunch of frickin' geniuses." His eyes dark with irritation, he caught Grady's in the rearview mirror, then twisted his head sharply to the left. "Hey, let me in, asshole!" Successfully merged, he leaned back. "Yep. Charlie—genius and fake sister, all in one."

Charlie giggled. "I'm not *fake*, you dummy!" She turned to the back seat. "Jess is always *saying* that. But Mama and Daddy's adopting me soon as the paper and court stuff's done. We're gonna have a party and everything and Jess is coming, too, because he'll be my *brother*." Watching her grin go megawatt, Grady could pretty much guess who was President, Vice President, Secretary, and Treasurer of the Official Jess Williams Fan Club. Then she grew serious and let Grady and Pearl in on a big secret. "Right now, I'm a foster."

"What you are," Jess muttered, "is a pain in the butt."

The light in Charlie's eyes wavered, her face clouding over. "Am not."

Jess sighed. "Course not. In the sister department, you're everything I ever dreamed of."

Charlie's lower lip slid out. "Am—too." Confusion danced across her face.

Jess laughed and shook his head, braking for a light. "Like I said—genius."

Grady saw tears building in Charlie's eyes. Jess glanced at her and frowned, then leaned over and flicked a tear away with his finger. "Relax, kid—okay? You thrill me. Really." But more tears followed the first. Jess sighed, reached into his pocket and handed over his handkerchief. Grady, knowing just what it felt like, watched Charlie clumsily blot her face and nose. Jess studied the traffic behind them, then moved forward with the green light. He glanced at Charlie and shrugged. "Hey, you're okay—really. My one and only almost bona fide sibling."

Charlie, placated—tears and nose wiped but her face still damp and red—twisted around to face Grady and Pearl. "Jess and Darla's taking me to the movies next week for my birthday." She turned to Jess. "Right?"

"Right." He rolled his eyes at Grady in the mirror and drove on in silence. Charlie made a little knotted ghost out of Jess's handkerchief. Saying, "Wo-o-o, wo-o-o!" she showed it first to Jess, then to Grady and Pearl. Grady smiled at her. Then Jess's voice exploded in his ears. "Okay, white people—outta my car! We're here."

The library looked different, changed by this new approach.

They went inside, Jess hauling Charlie off to the children's room. Standing beside Pearl, Grady didn't know what to do, settled for running his fingers up and down the zipper on his jacket—a tiny train track, smooth and bumpy at once.

He watched Pearl unbutton her jacket, and realized she'd left her portfolio in Jess's car. He must be giving her a ride home. He sighed and let his fingers take another ride on the tiny train track on his jacket.

They sat down at a table.

"Okay." Jess cleared his throat. "The thing is, if we do the three portraits of Bean Head thing, I got to change him around. No way I'm spending all my time painting some white dude. Far be it from me to dis the melanin-challenged here at the table, but I spend my whole life kissing up, you know? So Bean has to be black. But this is a joint project, so we've got to show a *jointness of intention*. Therefore, if I do a black Grady, Pearl has to do a girl Grady. Makes sense, right?"

Remembering the business card Fred had given him, Grady reached into his pocket and touched it. His hand retreated quickly to his lap.

"See, we'll be like nouveau *artistes*. Knock Ms. Spencer dead with our concept." Jess pinched the end of his nose. "Man, I got a cold or something. And I gave my handkerchief to Charlie." He scrunched his face up. "Hope you don't go mushy on me today, Bean Head. I'm fresh out of snot cloth." He looked at Pearl. "Got a tissue? Preferably gunk-free."

She dug in her pocket. "Of course," Jess continued, "that leaves Grady doing a Grady Grady, which basically means a skinny black line drawn straight down the middle of a piece of paper. A charcoal *masterpiece*. Our grade will definitely suffer." He took the tissue Pearl offered, examined it, then used it on his nose. "Or maybe we can recruit somebody else to do Grady's Grady."

He laughed, his eyes teasing. "I know—how about Fred?"

Grady pushed his chair back—it was time to go, get away, leave *now*—but something touched his wrist, surprising him into stillness. A small, hard, crinkly object slid into his hand. A peppermint, wrapped in cellophane. His fingers grappled with it hungrily, consuming its properties of roundness and hardness, its smoothness, all but devouring it with his fingertips. Pearl smiled at him shyly.

Jess resumed control. "So, okay. We invite Fred into our little family of artistes, and do a black Grady, a girl Grady, and a homo Grady. That's a full house, in my opinion. We'll probably place first in the spring art show. I'll even be absolved of homophobia."

He watched Grady's fingers work his peppermint.

"Man, I could use one of those. Did the taco bit again today. Darla's got this thing for Mexican." Pearl sent one spinning across the table, a red-and-white striped hockey puck. "Thanks." Jess unwrapped it, stuck it in his mouth. "So what do you guys think?"

Pearl unwrapped a peppermint for herself, the cellophane crinkling.

"I'm currently open for conversation." Jess sucked his mint, prodding. "I mean, I've got two ears, I can handle it."

"Um." Pearl started to speak, then stopped. Grady followed her stare.

No.

His body tensed, burst into flight—becoming sky, becoming air, becoming nothing.

Jess turned around. "Oh, there you are. I wondered when you guys would show up. Hey, Tracy, nice to see you again." Then, "I'm Jess. That's Pearl. And that, of course, is Grady, although I guess he's thinned out a bit since the last time you saw him. And you're—?"

Grady shut his eyes, listening.

"Ted."

"Right," Jess said. "I wasn't sure which one of you would be coming."

Grady opened his eyes. Tracy hesitated, taking the chair next to Jess, her face scrambled with emotion. Ted pulled a chair over from an adjacent table.

He was taller, a bit bulkier, his hair pretty much the same—dark, not too long, not too short, curly. But his face had changed; he looked older or something. Maybe handsomer. That was it. Ted had gone from merely good-looking to handsome. But his eyes, a pale hazel, seemed to struggle to contain something, and Grady realized the something was *him*. Ted was trying to see *him*, contain *him*, and was failing—the Grady he knew was nowhere in sight.

Jess cleared his throat, his eyes prodding Grady's nervously. "Yeah. Well, see, I got to talking to Tracy in the parking lot after you went psycho on us last Friday, and she told me about all your friends and stuff at your old school, so I thought—hey, reunion time. I mean, why not?"

Grady couldn't speak. A bird, huge and black, waited to devour him.

Jess tried again. "See, me and Tracy talked on the phone to arrange it, agree on terms. I thought a whole bunch of guys showing up at once might put you over the edge, make you go *double* psycho. So we settled on a one-person-at-a-time addition—and bam! Done. Right?" He looked to Tracy for confirmation.

She nodded, her eyes darting from Grady to Pearl, settling, helpless, on Ted.

Nobody spoke.

Pearl's mouth was pursed, her face tightened with guilt. "Um, Jess called me last night, and told me about Tracy. And your other friends. I thought it might be a good thing. If you saw them again. That it might, uh, help."

Help.

In the darkness swimming up through her eyes, swimming toward the surface, Grady knew that the help she meant was for the *Night Of*. Their conversation hadn't been a dream, she'd heard him clearly. He'd never be able to take it back.

"Grady." Tracy spoke quietly, her face flushed. "We just want to know what's wrong, that's all. I mean, if you really don't want to talk to us, or see us, fine. It's just—we need to know that you're okay." She stopped, tears wetting her cheeks.

"We couldn't get to you." Ted stared quietly into Grady's face. "I mean, your parents wouldn't even talk to me, your mother told me some phony story about a relative dying. Shit, Grady. I've known you for years. I was in your house all the time. We were *buddies*. You owed it to me, to tell me what was going on." Grady saw pain walk across Ted's face, his eyes bright, and in that moment Grady realized that Ted had lived an entire year without him—without *him*—and that everything they might have done together had been lost, forever. He wanted to throw back his head and howl.

Instead, he sat frozen. "I, um." He could barely move his lips. "S-sorry. Am."

"Yeah, well, like I said, Bean's still working on his verbal skills. Every time he says a whole sentence, he gets an M&M. The kind with nuts." Jess all but poked Grady with his eyes.

"I—"

Charlie walked up. "Got to go to the bathroom." She waved at Grady and Pearl, and that's when Grady discovered he was clutching Pearl's hand. Christ! How had that happened? He let go quick, his palm damp.

"So do it." Jess said, irritated. "Since when do you need an escort?"

Charlie shrugged, wrinkling her nose and sniffing at Jess's face. "Can I have a candy, too?"

Jess rolled his head toward Pearl, giving her a see-what-I-have-to-live-with look, and Pearl sent another peppermint spinning across the table. Jess handed it to Charlie.

"Thanks," she said, unwrapping it slowly. She stuck it in her mouth, smacking her lips and grinning. "You said I wasn't supposed to go anywhere."

"That doesn't include the bathroom, moron." Jess shook his head. "Down the hall, kid, and *quick*. I'm not wiping pee up off of the floor."

She giggled. "Okey-dokey, Jessie-jokey." She turned and walked away, stopping to swing a rack of paperbacks around before continuing on.

Jess shook his head. "Man." He turned to Tracy and Ted. "Well, as you can see, Grady has these psycho moments and his verbal skills are basically retarded. But his brain works. So maybe the next time you come, he'll actually put a whole sentence together. I've heard him do it. Just last night, matter of fact. He was telling me about—" He stopped. "Well, never mind. But the Bean can surprise you sometimes. Right, O Mighty Mental One?" His brown eyes tried to push their way in, but Grady resisted.

Ted nodded, slowly, but didn't look convinced. He turned to Tracy. "Well, maybe we should go." She nodded, half-smiled, and stood up.

"Yeah, I gotta go, too. You ready, POearl?" Jess yawned. "That's my life, driving people around. A large portion of 'em white. Makes you wonder, don't it?" He stood up and stretched. "Charlie probably ended up in the men's room or something. She's not exactly headed for West Point, you know?" He pulled his

Grady felt Pearl's reluctance to leave. His hand, dried on his jeans, still felt odd from holding hers, still felt hot and held. He didn't understand how it had happened.

Pearl pulled her jacket on. "Can I call you tonight?"

Grady nodded. Because he might not even be there, he still had to leave, run away. Tonight or some other night before next Tuesday. The day before his appointment with Dr. Hawthorne.

Ted spoke. "Grady? Jess told us you wait for your father to pick you up, but I can give you a ride home. It's right on our way."

Grady froze. Sit with them, knowing what they wanted to know, the question they needed answered—what *happened* to him? Impossible. He swallowed. "No. I mean, thanks."

Ted nodded and shrugged, his eyes darkening.

"Well, you can at least walk your ass out to the car. I mean, they drove clear across the county to see you, and I didn't exactly play a small role in this reunion thing of yours. I conducted the whole fucking *orchestra*. You could show a little gratitude, be all you can be instead of just being a jerk with a butthole for a brain." Jess glared, hot.

Walk out with them? But maybe that wasn't so bad. People did that all the time—walked in, walked out. He could do that.

Red and yellow leaves crunched under their feet as they walked down the sidewalk, the chilly air invading every crack in Grady's clothing.

Jess and Charlie and Tracy quickly packed distance, Jess yakking it up with Tracy, probably giving her an update on Grady's M&M consumption. So far: zero.

Pearl and Ted slowed down, keeping pace with Grady. They stopped together at the edge of the parking lot, nobody saying anything. Then Ted looked pointedly at Pearl, and her face went red. "Um," she said. "I'll, uh." She gave Grady a small, embarrassed shrug, then moved ahead alone.

"So." Ted looked at the curb, at the cars parked in front of them. "The whole Group wanted to come today. Hell, I would have been at your place last Friday night in a fast second, but Tracy said no." He shrugged, his nose turned slightly pink by the chill. "I didn't really believe her. About the way you are, I mean." They watched a squirrel dart its way across the parking lot. "What's going on?"

Grady's fingers took a train ride on his jacket. "I, um. Nothing. I mean, going on."

Ted's mouth tightened and he looked away. "Okay, then." The green in his eyes muddied, he stepped off the curb, heading toward the others.

Grady shivered and closed his eyes.

When he opened them again, the others stood in the empty parking space next to Jess's car. Pearl watched him, wanting him to follow. Jess and Tracy still talked, Ted standing slightly off to himself, looking away. Charlie butted her head into Jess's back, then turned and bobbed up and down in her own private boogie.

Grady swung his foot off the curb, letting his other foot follow.

Jess turned at his approach. "There he is. The Bean takes his first step for mankind." He rattled his car keys. "Okay, kiss everybody goodbye now. Till next time and all that. This black boy's gotta run. Damn it, Charlie, cut it out!"

Charlie head-butted him again and he grabbed her around the neck, holding her under his arm. "Man. This kid's gonna grow up to be a sumo wrestler or something."

Charlie giggled. "What's sumo?"

"That means you're big and fat and ugly and sit on people." Jess rapped her on the skull, then turned to Tracy and Ted. "Don't worry about Grade. I mean, you guys look like Western Civilization just ended, and you missed the last bus out. But I tell you, he's making progress."

Charlie wiggled out from under his arm, her hair looking like a haystack after a tornado. Ted touched Tracy on the shoulder. As they turned to leave, Grady's hand moved into the air—his second wave goodbye of the day.

"So, is this a private party?"

Leaning against the car parked on the other side of the Reliant, Gwendolyn smiled broadly, then strolled around to join them. She held a stack of papers against her chest, her jacket black and sleek, her red hair fluttering out from behind her ears with the breeze. She laughed. "I saw you guys in the library having this big powwow, so I didn't come over and say hi."

"O, break my heart." Jess rolled his eyes.

"I was doing some research, had to make a bunch of copies of something." She lifted the stack of papers in her arms, and one flew off, flapped against the ground and rolled. Pearl leaned down and grabbed it, started reading. "I've got this big, two-part article coming out in the paper. You know. The guys raping guys thing."

Gwendolyn looked at Ted and laughed. "Great subject, huh?" Her eyes, liking what they saw, teased—playing ball. "You don't go to Jefferson. Where're you from?"

Ted glanced at Grady, took in Jess's disdain. He settled for a careful shrug. "Delmont."

"Oh. I've seen your paper there. The *Banner*, right? It's better than it used to be, don't you think? At Jefferson we're doing some real cutting-edge reporting, like my two-part article." She laughed, trying to tame her breeze-blown hair. "Well, the first part's done, of course—that'll be out next Tuesday. That's the general information half. I got some stuff off the Internet. The second part will be in the next issue."

"Yeah, well you can shove your article, both parts, up your ass." Jess's eyes smoldered.

"Honestly, Jess. Grow up, would you?" She snorted in disgust, then looked at Ted. "The *Sentinel* at Claggett High picked up a story I did on possible food contamination in the cafeteria here, and ran a story on their own school. I'm sure one of the papers will take off on *this* subject, too, but I'll be there first. Right now, I'm researching the second part, looking for case histories. No names used, of course." She smiled at Grady, her eyes celebrating a quiet triumph. "I think I've found the most interesting new student of all."

Birds screamed in Grady's ears. He had to leave, run away *right now*—but Pearl's hand clamped down on his arm and he stopped, sweat flooding his skin. Then Pearl let go and moved toward Gwendolyn, the piece of paper crumpled in her fist.

"*What do you think you're doing?*" she shrieked. Grady backed up against the car behind him.

Gwendolyn arched her eyebrows in amusement. "Excuse me?"

"You—you creep! You horrible person! You—you're nothing but a terrible, horrible person." She waved the piece of paper. "If you use this, I'll—you'll pay! If you use this, you'll be sorry, I'll make you sorry!"

Gwendolyn smirked. "Oh, my," she said. "They let you out of your cage a day early, don't you think?" She laughed. "It's public information, *Pearl*. So I'll use it."

Pearl barreled dead ahead, shoving Gwendolyn against the car parked on the other side of the empty space. Direct hit. Bull's-eye.

Gwendolyn, stunned, released a mighty *oomph* from her lungs, flailing against the car as Pearl tried to rip the papers out of her arms. They struggled, a flurry of shoving elbows and flying hair, red and dark. Jess grabbed Charlie, hauling her out of the way.

Oh jeez. Oh shit. Grady clung to the side of Jess's car, trembling and sick to his stomach, as Pearl continued her assault on Gwendolyn's arms. Then the papers were loose, landing in a thump on the asphalt, picking themselves up and tumbling briskly away. But Pearl kept shoving her body into Gwendolyn's, tearing at her jacket. "Stop it!" Gwendolyn screamed, tears spilling down her cheeks. "Stop it! Stop it!"

Grady was moving, he didn't know how. He grabbed Pearl by the back of her coat and pulled. She was a weight he could barely handle, how had he gotten so weak? Jess jumped in, cramming himself between the two girls to shove them apart. Grady pulled harder and Pearl finally peeled away—a barnacle detached.

Gwendolyn's hair was wild, her face red. "You stupid bitch!" she yelled. "You *attacked* me! You ruined my jacket! You're crazy— all of you, you're crazy. I'm reporting you, I'm calling the police right now! On all of you!" She turned to run toward the library, but Jess grabbed her by the arm, jerked her back and held her.

"Excuse me. *Gwendolyn*."

He spun her around and backed her up against his car. "Okay, Barbie doll, *relax*. Do the take-five bit." He glanced at Grady, then cleared his throat and smiled at Gwendolyn. "You see, in my opinion, it's clear that Grady and me just saved your butt from being made into succotash by Pearl." His eyes danced merrily across Gwendolyn's face. "Hey, she surprised me, too. I didn't think she had it in her. I guess this female sumo shit is really catching on." He laughed.

"And, no bull about it—she attacked you first, she was in the wrong. And I'm a fucking *authority* on wrong, okay? But this calling in the cops business is just plain crap. Unwarranted and all that. Because once you add in the bitch factor, Pearl's totally justified in her actions. You win Bitch Gold every time. So, what I think—since me and Grade did the hero bit and saved you from the Wrath of Pearl—is that you owe us." He waited, not letting her escape his dark eyes.

Gwendolyn pushed her hair behind her ears, trying to regain composure. "I don't think so."

"Well, I do." He waited. "See, I happen to know I'm not the only one who's engaged in what you might call extracurricular activity in the classroom—you know, after school, when the teacher's stepped away. Now, if my memory serves me correctly, room 107 is where the paper is put together, right? Well, I happen to know of a certain red-headed reporter—whose name, I think, is Gwendolyn—who's been known to entertain a certain blond reporter, right in that very same room. What's that guy's name? Oh, right. Bruce."

Gwendolyn's eyes flashed. "That's a lie!"

Jess laughed. "Really? Let's just say I have my sources. Like you, I know how to find things out." He smirked and stepped back. "Well, you know, people talk, that's just a fact. People say *I* got a mouth problem, but you should hear Bruce. But, hey, don't worry—I haven't spread it around, not really. I'm not that kind of guy. I say go for it, get your rocks off. But you know how teachers get themselves all worked up when they find out it's going on in a classroom, you know? Shit, even I know that stuff like that can get you thrown off a paper."

He shrugged, his dark eyes smiling, and Gwendolyn's face tightened. Furious, she shoved her way past Jess, stopping to pick up what was left of her papers.

"Oh," he added. "One more thing. Whatever Pearl was talking about—about you using something? Don't do it, okay?" Gwendolyn straightened up and looked at him. He smiled. "We got everything settled now?" Loving his advantage.

Gwendolyn jerked her shoulder and stormed past the lot of them, heading for the other side of the parking lot. Grady realized a bunch of people were standing around looking at them. A few kids from Jefferson, a couple of mothers with strollers, an old guy peering over his glasses.

Jess laughed. "Been waiting to use that. Thank you, *Bruce*. Damn, I'm a happy man." He waved and smiled at the small crowd. "Party's over, folks. Just a little wrestling exhibition, female sumo division. They're aiming for the nationals, but frankly, they're not there yet." He waved his hands again and people started to move away.

Grady's fingers sought the train track on his jacket—cold and hard, taking him away.

Ted picked up one of the papers Gwendolyn had dropped. Jess reached down, picked another one up. "So what's she working on, anyway?"

Grady looked at Pearl's red, tear-streaked face. When had she started crying? She numbly handed him the piece of paper wadded up in her fist. With a rush of anxiety, he flattened it out.

The article in the paper. The one Gwendolyn had heard him mention to Fred, the one written almost a year ago, about a young man who'd been raped on the first Friday night in November. He'd been sixteen years old, but gee gosh golly, why hadn't he defended himself? After all, he was six foot three, had a good build, he'd weighed—

A black vortex roared through his head; he couldn't stand up any longer, he was falling.

* * *

He sat on the ground, his back against the side of Jess's car, a blur of faces staring at him. Heat penetrated his side—Pearl, sitting beside him, pressed close, her arm tucked through his. How long had they been sitting there? Everyone else was standing up.

Tracy leaned close, her hand on his chin, her eyes frightened. She straightened up and he saw Ted, his face tight with shock and disbelief.

And Jess, his face indecipherable.

"What's this mean?" Charlie asked, trying to read one of the copies.

"Nothing." Jess grabbed the paper out of her hands and crumpled it up.

"Well, then—" Charlie wiggled her way under Jess's arm. "How come everybody's so quiet now? And I'm *cold*."

"Yeah, well, the earth's gonna burn up in five million years, so enjoy the cooler temperatures now, okay?" Jess shook her off, walking around to the back of his Reliant. Grady felt the trunk open and shut, saw Jess bring back a mangy blanket and dump it on Charlie. "Here, have a blast." Charlie wrapped herself up in it, giggling. "I'm a burrito!"

"No shit."

They sat or stood in silence. A few people glanced at them as they headed into or out of the library. Grady felt a leaden chill creep into his body, but his left side stayed warm from Pearl. Nobody spoke, nobody moved until Jess finally jumped up and down. "Mr. West!" he yelled. "Over here!"

Grady's father came over, surprise outlining his face as he recognized Ted and Tracy. But when he saw Grady, he grew alarmed. "Are you okay?" He reached down, helping him to his feet. Pearl helped too, her arm still tucked under Grady's, not letting go.

Ted, his face white, his eyes blazing, finally spoke. "You owe me, Mr. West!" he shouted. "You owe me, big!"

EIGHT

Grady and his father rode home in silence, Ted's words, furious and unforgiving, reverberating through the car—"Why didn't you tell me—*me*—what happened? I was Grady's friend. Didn't that mean anything?" Grady's father sagged behind the wheel as he drove, his face lined with misery. But really, what could he have done a year ago? What could he have said?

Grady closed his eyes. Some hells just can't be shared.

He walked quietly into the living room, the glowing dial of his watch clutched in his hand. 2:06 A.M. The couch and chairs and television were dark blobs, but he knew his way. He lay on the couch, reaching for the throw his mother kept across the back. Might as well be warm. The room settled over him like a bird sheltering its brood.

He jerked awake, pulling his watch up to his eyes. 2:22. Jeez. Friday morning was almost here. He turned on his side, the sofa cushions strange and lumpy.

He jerked awake, grappling with the throw. 2:31. Jesus. His eyelids felt as heavy as sandbags, his exhaustion a river he couldn't contain. And yet—

He jerked awake, his body jarred by the impact. 2:43. This was ridiculous. He stared at the ceiling, willing his eyes to stay open.

Everybody knew. All of them knew.

He sat up, leaning forward, dangling like a puppet on a loose string. At some point, he lay back down, a puppet with the string cut.

He jerked awake. 3:19.

They knew.

Tears flowed down his face. They knew.

The smell of oatmeal nudged him out of sleep. Sitting up on the couch, he numbly took the bowl his mother handed him. At least it wasn't soup.

Dark circles under her eyes, his mother stood, wrapped in her robe, smelling of coffee. "That girl called again last night. Pearl. But you were asleep, I didn't want to wake you." She waited in awkward silence for a response, but he gave none. "I'm, uh, glad you got to see Ted and Tracy again. I always liked them. The whole Group, I mean." Embarrassed, she ran her fingers through her clipped blonde hair. "Well, I've got to go get my shower." She left, not mentioning the most important fact of all, that they *knew*.

Grady picked up the spoon, then set it back down.

Jess sat beside him in homeroom, but didn't quite look at him. His eyes made a fast landing on Grady's face, then took off, quick. But that was fine. Grady didn't want Jess to look at him. He'd forgotten to run away last night, he had to tend to that this weekend. He watched Jess fill up an entire page in his composition book with cross marks, hatches, and doodles.

At lunch, Grady sat outside by himself at the picnic table next to the Dumpster. An open, rock-hard chocolate Dixie cup occupied the space in front of him, untouched. He was freezing, but at least he was alone. He closed his eyes.

The table wobbled. Jess and Darla, bundled up in jackets, sat down across from him. Grady looked down, hiding his shame, but knew that Darla could see it anyway. Jess fidgeted uncomfortably, finally grabbing the Dixie cup. He hacked away with the small scoop, sliding hard chocolate chunks into his mouth, and when he had finished, stood up. "See you in art, Bean. Okay?"

Okay.

Sitting beside him, Pearl offered him one M&M after another—the kind without nuts. He refused them, letting her slip them into her own mouth. Finally he took one, blue, carefully cracking the thin candy shell with his teeth, letting the pieces collapse and dissolve, letting the chocolate envelop his tongue.

Jess thrust his opened palm toward Pearl, demanding his share.

Fred, officially divorced from Gwendolyn, now sat at a different table with a couple of other kids. Another three-person portrait in the making. Gwendolyn, her anger smoldering on her face like a brush fire, also sat with others. So now there were three, three-person portraits in process. Ms. Spencer walked around the room, mostly looking pissed.

Jess gathered his Wild Things paintings together, started laying in words. "One night Max put on his space suit and kicked butt. His mother called him Wild Thing, and he said, 'Fuck off, Earth Bitch.' That night a space ship landed and Max took command, flew to the planet Africa, home of the really wild mutha—." He stopped writing, looking flustered, then crumpled the entire picture up into a wad and shoved it across the table. Started in on the next one.

Grady filled his own piece of paper with the color black, leaving a small, white rectangle at the top, where he wrote in the title. *Charcoal.*

"Shit," Jess muttered, tearing up another page.

When class ended, Grady walked to the public library, refusing Jess's offer of a ride, refusing Pearl's anxious eyes. He made his way alone, jumping every time a loud car or truck passed. He had to get over that.

Saturday morning, Grady got up at nine and nibbled around the edges of a Pop Tart, ignoring the scrambled eggs and bacon his mother brought to him. He slid IIIrd Tyme Out into his CD player, and began to plot his official running away from home.

He'd take his portable player, bluegrass CDs, scissors to keep his hair cut short. But no razor—a beard might be good, no one would recognize him. Extra shirt and pair of jeans. A couple pairs of underwear. Socks. He had a little money, not much, but he'd take what he had. Pencils, for his fingers. He'd have to find other surfaces along the way.

And maybe some M&Ms, he'd stop to buy a pack. He closed his eyes, already wiped.

When he woke up, the Group stood crowded beside his bed. Not just sad Tracy and angry Ted, but also Mikey-Mike, his pale face shocked, and Christian, swallowing hard and holding Tracy's hand. And Clara-bell, with her classic breasts.

Was this a dream? Had to be.

Nobody knew, they didn't.

Grady closed his eyes and turned over, pulling a pillow over his head.

He woke up.

Jess sat next to his bed, dreads falling forward as he scribbled away in his composition book, half a grilled cheese sandwich in his left hand. Charlie sat on the floor, chewing on her own sandwich, earnestly wearing a red crayon down to the nub in a coloring book.

Grady's father entered the room and set a tray beside his bed. A grilled cheese sandwich. Plus a cup of vegetable soup and a box of crackers.

His father looked at Charlie. "Mrs. West said she's ready to add the chocolate chips to the cookie dough. You want to come help her?"

His mother was baking cookies? *Homemade* cookies? Homemade *chocolate chip* cookies? He must be closer to death than he realized. Charlie smiled shyly and nodded, looked at Jess.

Jess tilted his head toward the door. "Just keep your fingers out of the dough, okay? No one wants to eat anything *your* stumps have been digging in." Charlie giggled and followed Mr. West down the hall.

Jess watched her leave, then thumped his pen against his notebook, his mouth twisted down. "That Charlie? The one about to booger-up your mom's recipe? Everybody thinks it's so great that I do stuff with her. Big black brother and little white sister, right? Even my *dad* thinks it's great—like we're a living episode of Race, the Final Frontier—soon to be released on video." He shook his head.

"But I only do stuff with Charlie because I can't *not* do it, you know? I mean, she thinks I'm her *brother*, for Christ's sake. But I'm not." He drew a vicious doodle in his book. "Not not not!" Anger slid across his face like a dark cloud. "So you see, Grady-man, you aren't the only one with a problem."

He studied Grady, his eyes serious. "Enough of *my* happy life, though." He reached for a saltine. "Your mama's getting real nervous about you, Grade. Got the car already warmed up and pointed toward that Hawthorne guy. Although I have to say the skinny junkie look is in. Pick up a habit and a tattoo and you'll be set."

Grady took a cracker, snapping off a bite.

"So, Fred knows about this, um, rape stuff? That's what he was talking about Thursday afternoon, right? You told him about it."

Grady could hear the hurt in Jess's voice. "Sort of. He, um, figured it out."

"Well, okay." Jess half-shrugged. "All right." Silence. "I looked it up on the Internet." Grady remained silent. "That's some pretty crazy shit, Bean."

Grady tried to breathe.

"And the weird part?" Jess studied the ceiling. "Most of the guys who do that kind of thing are straight. You'd figure them for, you know, fags. I mean—gay. Predisposed toward guys. But"— Jess's eyes landed on Grady's face, then skittered away—"that's not the way it is. Made me lose *my* appetite. Made me real sad to be a skinny little colored boy." He twisted his dreads in his fingers. "You all right with this?"

Grady nodded dumbly. He finished the cracker, listening as Jess's voice said something about men—the violent kind, at least—using sex to establish domination over other men. Or some-thing like that. A kind of testosterone pecking order, maybe— complete with getting your rocks off. Not a bad deal for those of the criminal persuasion.

But Jess's words became a blur. It was more than Grady could take in. He numbly picked up another saltine.

"Shit," said Jess, "if *I* wanted to prove I was the biggest, baddest dude in the land, for sure I'd come up with a better plan than that. I mean, Jesus."

Grady put the cracker down, leaning back on his pillows. Jess himself became a blur.

* * *

"Pearl called." His mother handed him a bowl of cream of tomato. Were they trying to kill him? He top-loaded it with saltines.

Sitting up in bed, building a soggy cracker mountain, he remembered sticking Pearl's phone number under his phone. The same place he'd stuffed the card Fred had given him.

Two numbers he couldn't use.

On Sunday afternoon, Ted spent five awkward minutes sitting with Grady, both of them silent. Ted's unhappy eyes darted from Grady's face to the floor to the ceiling, as Grady's fingers worked overtime on the underside of the TV tray beside his bed. Then Ted stood up, exited, and spent five more minutes in the living room yelling at Grady's father.

Grady didn't know how to make anyone feel better.

It was weird, though—everybody knew, yet no one had asked about the actual rape. No one had asked for a single detail about what really happened to him. And that was good, because there was no way he'd ever tell.

And yet.

He felt like his own continent, surrounded by water no one was willing to cross. He'd been so frightened of everybody's knowing, but now their silence stretched into the distance like a cold, dark sea.

Cold and deep.

Sunday evening Grady took a call from Pearl. "You okay?" she asked, her voice small. "Yes," he mumbled. "You?" His fingers explored the quilt on his bed. Soft. As soft and mushy as crackers in warm soup. "Um, yes," she answered. He said nothing. She finally uttered an embarrassed, "Well, bye then," and hung up, the unspoken words between them a silence that stretched for aeons, maybe ending somewhere in the next universe.

Where they would no doubt talk for hours, Grady telling her all about his night in the van.

"We'll make do," Ms. Spencer announced, a little too cheer-
fully, as they filed into their temporary classroom. "Creating art,"
she said, "is hard. There's never a guarantee of either shelter or
success."

"I'd settle for a guarantee of no dead frogs," muttered Jess.
"Damn, it stinks." He thumped his books down on the skinny lab
table. Grady sat next to him. Pearl hesitated, then took the seat
next to his.

Same time. Same game. Different smell.

Which was precisely why he had signed up for Botany instead
of Biology: dead little animals preserved in formaldehyde. He
thought of Bad Bud.

"We'll have our room back by tomorrow. This will be a good
opportunity to learn more about each other."

"How?" Jess muttered. "By examining each other's animal
nature? Booty in Biology?"

Ms. Spencer dumped a load of supplies on the desk at the
front of the room. "This can't be helped."

Early that morning, the girls' bathroom down the hall from
the art rooms had basically imploded and hurled, sending water
roiling like a river across linoleum and under classroom doors.
Things were cleaned up, more or less, but the wing was still
contaminated or something. Men were at work in the girls' room—
in the distance you could hear drills and banging.

"Your projects are fine. Thank goodness nothing above the

floor was touched or ruined." Ms. Spencer beamed. "Today we'll just do a still life. As you can see, they're all set up."

Theirs was a pear and one of those petrified ears of corn people use for decoration in the fall. Jess reached for the pear, then stopped. "Forget it. It probably tastes like something dead. I tell you, all the fun has gone out of art." He left to get paper and pieces of charcoal.

Grady glanced at Pearl. She was busy ignoring him, her lips furled tightly in a hurt silence. He hadn't exactly been Mr. Boyfriend on the phone last night.

Jess slid paper in front of each of them, dropping sticks of charcoal. Pearl nodded her thanks to Jess, but continued to ignore Grady. She picked up her charcoal and got to work.

Well, thanks a lot, Miss Snot. Like she had twenty boyfriends waiting in line. And why'd she wear that rose-colored T-shirt again? With jeans, it made her look like she had this *body*. Didn't she know her stupid T-shirt made her look—well, like she had *breasts*?

Jess started drawing, stopped, then flipped his sheet of paper over and began writing something. More *Muthafucka Stories*?

Frustrated, Grady flicked his eyes around the room. Charts and lab equipment were everywhere. He *hated* science. Gwendolyn sat at a table way at the other end of the room. Fred was up front.

What was it with clothes today, anyway? Was it National Get Out of Bed and Put on Something Hot Day? Fred wore a dark brown pullover that came damn close to matching the color of his hair. Did he dress that way on purpose, so people would say, *Oh, look, there's Mr. Handsome*? Just how many homos per square inch did he think lived around here?

Grady closed his eyes, willing everything away. When he opened them, everything was still there.

He picked up his piece of charcoal and began drawing. Under his skilled hands, the corncob and pear began to reveal their true shape and meaning: a short, stumpy roll of paper towels sporting an Indian headdress, and a funky breast with a nipple. But, hey— once he was gone, a runaway or just plain dead, this picture would be worth millions. A Grady West *Experience*.

The bell rang. Class was over.

Nobody at their table moved. Why didn't Jess take his picture, why didn't he and Pearl leave? Grady closed his eyes, fiddling with the air moving in and out of his lungs. It stunk, but what else could you expect around dead animals? Someone pulled a stool over from the next lab station.

Fred.

He sat down cautiously, his eyes on full defense, holding Jess at a careful distance. He turned to Grady. "That number any help?"

Grady flushed. "Um, no."

"Oh." Fred glanced away, then looked back and shrugged. "Okay, then. Sorry." He started to get up.

"Didn't call."

"What number?" Jess might give Fred the space and distance he demanded, but not the whole room.

Grady's fingers plunged to his lap. "Um." Fred's eyes darted from him to Jess and back again, uncertain.

"For Allan Reeve, at the Men's Health Center." There, a virtual proclamation. Was it night yet? He needed sleep.

"On that card you gave him?" Jess's eyes measured Fred, testing. "So who's Allan Reeve, and what's the Men's Health Center? What's it do?"

Fred's eyes maintained position. "Do?"

"It's about the rape thing, right? That's why you gave it to him."

Birds flew screaming at him out of the sky, Grady had to duck, dodge, they would tear his eyes out, rip his skin open—why couldn't anyone else see them? They were starving, looking for flesh, looking for meat, looking for blood—

Fred cleared his throat. "Yeah."

"So what's the deal?" Special Agent Jess sprang into action, his eyes conducting a full search of Fred's face, seeking out weapons, hidden agendas.

Fred shrugged. "I go to this place for gay teens, and one of the counselors there said this Reeve guy at the Men's Health Center would be a good person for someone like Grady to talk to."

"So what's the Men's Health Center?" Jess continued his scrutiny.

Fred kept his attention focused on Jess. "It's a place for gay men to get health services. But this guy will talk to other people, too. I mean, it's not like we're under quarantine." He shrugged. "Maybe he can tell Grady—how to get help."

The help Grady needed most was for this conversation to end.

"Grady, you should do it. I mean, call." Pearl had finally decided he was worth talking to. Thank you so much. But why'd she have to say *that*? Grady squeezed his eyes shut, willing this to pass.

Pearl's hand touched his own, under the table. He opened his eyes. Jesus. She was holding his *hand*. Still, he didn't resist, didn't pull away. Didn't look at her, either. He found his fingers lightly caressing hers. What did they smell like—peppermints or chocolate or licorice? A candy girl, that's what she was. He felt her knuckles. Fingers were like pencils in a way—hard, containing bone.

"Well, look who the fuck it is." Jess folded his arms, glaring.

"My, what a cozy little group." Gwendolyn stood next to their table, her eyes hostile. "Let's see, the homophobic black guy, the gay guy, the *raped* guy." She laughed. "Not that I would spread that around about you, Grady. You know what people do with rumors." Her eyes, cold as glass, cut from him to Jess, then flickered back to Pearl. "And the girl in search of a diet." She snorted. "So what did you and Fred do, Jess? Kiss and make up?

But I guess kissing would have a whole new meaning in this group."

"You bitch." Jess stood up, tight with anger, his voice low. He leaned forward, clenching his fists on the table. Fred glanced at Grady, then rose, pushing his stool behind him. Time to go.

"Don't."

Gwendolyn swung her eyes to Grady, they all did. "Excuse me?"

"D-don't."

She laughed. "Don't what?"

"Tell. P-please." Grady tried to keep the tears out of his eyes. Jesus. He was *begging*. Pearl tightened her hand over his.

"Man. This is crap." Jess shoved his stool behind him with his foot, his voice going nuclear. "You keep your mouth shut about Grady, you got that?" Ms. Spencer, across the room talking to some kids, jerked her head up.

Oh, jeez. Grady gripped Pearl's hand. Gwendolyn would talk, everyone in school would know, call him names, attack him—

Gwendolyn laughed. "So what are you going to do, Jess—hit me?" She tucked her hair behind her ears. "But don't worry. *I* wouldn't tell. *I* don't trample on other people's privacy." Her blue eyes strutting victory, she turned and walked away.

Jess, his face dark with fury, watched her go, then sat down on his stool with a thump.

Fred ran his fingers back through his hair. "God, what a bitch."

Jess looked at him with a new respect.

Fred studied Grady, his eyes intense with something Grady didn't understand. "Look," he said, "even if she does talk—so what? If you start to get okay with yourself, with what happened, you'll survive. Hell, everybody's been talking about *me* for years." He half-laughed. Then he shrugged, a bitter smile returning to his lips. "Well, you'll survive if you've got backup."

"Hey, *I'm* backup." Jess's eyes blazed.

"Right." Fred stood up, his eyes once more holding Jess at gunpoint—then he seemed to relent, lowering his weapon, letting him go. "Just watch who you fight, okay?" He lingered a moment on Jess's face, then turned to Grady. "If you want, maybe we can talk sometime."

Grady nodded and watched him leave. Who would he be meeting at his teen place, who were his friends? Did he have his own Group?

"Well, he's okay, I guess." Jess turned to Grady. "I mean, for a—oh, never mind." He frowned, thumping his thumbs against the table. "Man, I am sick to death of all this crap. And I'm *hungry*. Wanna go get a bite?"

A *bite*? Grady almost laughed out loud, then realized he was thirsty. A Coke would be good, he could get that down. Or—what about a milk shake, a chocolate milk shake? *Milk shake*? That was crazy, he'd never be able to—

He discovered Pearl's hand, still encased in his. Odd. His fingers began to waltz over her palm. Slowly, he enclosed her hand in his two hands. It felt like holding a bird, or—he almost laughed—Bad Bud. He turned to find Jess watching him, a quiet round of table drums in progress. "They"—he forced the words—"hurt me." A bird cried, it was hungry, searching for food.

Jess's thumbs banged out the end of his solo, and he nodded. "Guess so, Grady-man." His eyes held Grady's for a moment, then shifted away. He stretched, cracking his knuckles. "Well, I'm starving. If you want food, follow." He stood up, gathered their pictures together, and took them to Ms. Spencer.

Grady hesitated, then rose as well, letting go of Pearl's hand. No milk shake. He'd only get sick. A Coke might work. The fizz usually went down okay. Maybe—

He realized Pearl was still sitting, her rosebud lips shut tight with embarrassment. Didn't she know she was invited, too? How could he tell her?

His fingers galloped to a button. Smooth and cold, incredibly round. The next one—

It wasn't working, he needed a new surface, he needed—

He reached for Pearl's hand. She gave it, hesitant and uncertain, then stood up, curling her fingers around his. She reached to pick up her portfolio, turning with him to follow Jess out the door. Grady felt his face flush. He knew people could see him—a zip holding a girl's hand. But for some reason, he didn't care. In the distance, a bird cried again, tired and hungry.

Grady was tired, too. He wanted to live.

THIRTY

"Shit. It shoulda placed at least third." Jess flicked the pale green ribbon fastened to the bottom of their self-portrait of three people, disgusted.

"Honorable Mention is okay," Pearl said bravely, her voice trembling. Grady squeezed her hand. Last year she'd come in first at this same event, the Spring Art Show. They walked around the table to view the whole thing—three canvases wired together back-to-back to form a triangle, KID DREAD, BOY WONDER! written on a banner across the top.

The room was pretty crowded. Kids from all over the county had entered, and they had shown up, along with their parents and friends. Grady's parents were on the other side of the room, holding plastic cups filled with punch and talking to Jess's father. Jess's mom and Moby Dick were looking at sculptures over by the entrance.

"It's gotta be the judges, you know? They got Bad Attitude crammed up their butts. And they're prejudiced as hell, you can tell. Damn it, Charlie, I'm not a punching bag. Cut it out!" Jess shook Charlie off his arm. "Go get some cookies or something."

"Where?"

"Duh! At the table where it says Refreshments!" He rolled his eyes as Charlie grinned and bounced over toward the table. "And I gotta wait another year to leave for college? She's got this invisible pogo stick now. Don't even ask." Jess surveyed the room. "So where's—hey! Trace! Over here!"

The Group walked up.

Grady instinctively reached for a button, then made himself

stop, willing his fingers to relax. He still couldn't quite get over it, the way Ted and Mikey-Mike and Christian and Clara-bell and Tracy had loped back into his life, awkward and frightened and uncertain, but back.

Working with Dr. Hawthorne, he'd gained some weight. He wasn't close to what he used to be, *Before*, but he was closer. He'd let his hair grow back, a little. Pearl wanted to see what it looked like longer, but he wasn't ready for that, and maybe never would be. But she didn't push him, not on that or anything. They were moving toward something, but it was a slow walk.

Mr. Reeve—Allan—said that was fine, though. "Sometimes you just need a slow walk. There's no reason to rush anything." Fred's card had come in handy.

"I like it!" Tracy laughed, her blonde hair gleaming. Grady knew he'd never get over that—her blonde hair. His last remembrance of *Before*. But—he looked at Pearl, whose dark hair curled and shone on her shoulders. *After* was okay, too. *After* was actually pretty fine.

"So whose is whose?" Ted's hazel eyes crinkled with amusement. Like he couldn't guess.

"I've been looking all over for you. Is this the masterpiece?" Darla poked her head around Jess's shoulder. Jess turned and grinned. No slow walk for them.

Mikey-Mike laughed. "I still say we should have done a Group Grady."

"Three is enough, thank you." Everyone paused a moment and looked at him, then resumed chattering, milling around the table their piece sat on. They still weren't used to Grady talking much.

Darla circled the table and stopped in front of Jess's canvas. "Shoot, Jess. I could've done better than *that*."

After a fumbling start at painting a black Grady, Jess had finally switched to white, announcing, "What we don't need is fake black people." The figure, shown from the chest up, wearing a pale blue T-shirt with the words *Dread Till You Drop* on it, actually looked a little bit like Grady. But the hair was his masterpiece. Punching holes in the canvas to tie it in place, he had used black yarn twisted into ropes to give Grady a huge mountain of long black dreads.

"That's to show the influence of African-American culture on you white guys," he said. "I mean, are we not *dope*? Besides," he had grinned, looking at Grady, "it's time you did something about your hair."

That night Grady put the clippers away and set his follicles free. A *little* bit free.

On one side of Jess's Grady, the dreads flowed down to a small African-American figure he painted into the corner of the canvas. More holes punched in the canvas allowed him to shape fuzzy chains around the figure's neck and ankles.

"Nothing personal," he said. "But it's not like we don't know what happened, lo those many years ago, when folks *africanus blackus* got jiggy with America."

Pearl didn't make a girl Grady. He felt kind of overwhelmed by her portrait—she not only could draw, she could *paint*. On her own, she probably would have landed another First. But she'd gone with their three-person entry.

She had also painted him from the chest up, making him look pretty much the way he really did—except she made him sort of naked. Not naked as in no clothes, but naked as in no skin, at least on his chest. She'd grabbed the dreads on the other side of Jess's portrait and pulled them over to her own canvas. Knotting in more yarn, she curved a really long dread around Grady's head and over his shoulder to his open chest. Inside his chest she painted a huge red-and-blue heart broken into two pieces, like an eggshell. Out of the shell flew a bird, carrying in its beak a black strand of yarn.

He didn't know how she knew about the birds. He'd never told her about them.

Mikey-Mike, walking around the table, burst out laughing.

"Damn, Grady. Yours *stinks*."

A chortle started somewhere deep in Grady's gut, and Pearl started giggling. His canvas *did* stink.

Not having a clue what to paint, he'd waited until Jess and Pearl had finished theirs. Then, the day before deadline, he grabbed a hank of dreads from the middle of Jess's Grady and pulled them way over to *his* canvas. Knotting in more as Pearl had done, he shaped the yarn into a long, black stick figure and glued it to the canvas, giving it a round head with a fringe of dreads. Inside the head, he painted two blue dots for eyes, and a red curve for a mouth. Finis. It took about forty-five minutes.

"Yeah, well, we know where the Honorable Mention part came from," Jess muttered. He turned to Darla. "Without Grade we definitely would've nailed Second."

"So, is this the *installation*?"

Everyone turned at Fred's approach. "Hey," said Clara-bell, laughing. "Is there any other?" By now, even the Group had met Fred.

Grady still sometimes felt shy around him, even though they'd had some good conversations. Actually, they were even sort of friends. Okay, maybe they *were* friends. He didn't know why he felt odd sometimes. After an awkward beginning, he wasn't shy anymore around Mr. Reeve, and *he* was gay. With him, he mostly felt safe. Mr. Reeve suggested it was because Fred reminded him of some of his confusions. "But confusions," he'd said, "are pretty normal. They're *really* normal after what you've been through."

"Oh," said Fred to the Group. "This is Paul."

Paul, taller and thinner than Fred, his light brown hair streaked to a sunlit blond, nodded at everyone, his mouth curving into a wicked grin. "Is this where I get autographs?"

Grady had met Paul before, and so had Jess and Darla and Pearl. Jess had proved strangely receptive to him. "Well," he had finally said, rubbing his nose. "I guess the Homos have arrived. Far be it from me to greet them at the shore with chains."

If Fred was just "regular," Paul, well, wasn't. You couldn't put your finger on it, exactly. He didn't look so different or anything. He just shimmered in and out of focus, somehow.

Grady felt like he, himself, shimmered in and out of focus. But in and out of focus of *what*, he didn't know. Something still wasn't quite right.

"Well," Mr. Reeve had said, a while back, "maybe it's like that three-person portrait you're working on. Or in your case," he laughed, "not working on. You're just not *finished* yet."

Standing in front of his canvas, Grady felt himself blur. Then, feeling the weight of his own bones and blood, he came back. It was odd, having a body to return to.

He watched Charlie take aim at Jess and land a head-butt. "Damn it, Charlie! Would you stop it?" Jess grabbed her arms and held them up, holding her away. "Anybody wanna buy a kid for cheap?"

Grady laughed as Pearl leaned close, her warmth flooding his skin. For a moment, Grady let his own body heat flow back.

Mr. Reeve was right. He wasn't finished.

But he had begun.